A FENLAND MURDER

BY

NICO DOBBEN

About the author

Norfolk, and in particular, West Norfolk, has been the home of Nico Dobben after moving from the Netherlands in 1981. Since then he has worked in a variety of jobs including delivery driver, roadie, factory worker and teacher. His creative output has focussed mainly on song writing and performing. He has released two albums of original songs.

A Fenland Murder is his first novel.

Acknowledgements

I would like to thank Anne, Hannah, Janneke, Marie, Ruth and Terry for reading the first draft and giving me constructive feedback.

I also like to mention the role of Derek Paice and other members of the Downham Market Songwriters' and Poets' Club in indulging me by listening to my plans and encouraging me to continue writing.

Having been able to discuss the book and process of getting it published with Carole and Kerran has been a great help.

I am grateful for the suggestions offered by Helen and Bill Scott, the majority of which are included in this revised edition. Any remaining errors are, of course, entirely mine.

Finally, I would like to thank Abigail Frusher for the original artwork used on the cover.

Front cover painting: 'A Fenland Landscape' by Abigail Frusher

ISBN 978-1-914408-81-6

Printed by Biddles Book Printers
www.biddles.co.uk
Blackborough End, King's Lynn, Norfolk

Dedicated to all the crime writers whose books I
have enjoyed over the years.

PROLOGUE

If someone had told Jimmy Jackson he would be dead within forty-five minutes of getting up that morning he would have stayed in bed. But no one did so he rose before dawn, put on his overalls, retrieved the shotgun from the cabinet and made his way to the grain store. Breakfast could wait. If he was going to make any inroads on the rat population this was the best time of the day to do so. He entered the large shed but when he was about to turn on the lights and close the door he heard a car coming down the track.

MONDAY

1

The road from Downham Market to Wisbech runs along the Well Creek, a narrow Fenland river winding its way upstream from Downham Market to Outwell. It is on this road that Detective Chief Inspector Steve Culverhouse from the Special Fenland Police Force finds himself driving towards the village of Nordelph. The call had come in half an hour earlier that a body, most likely that of farmer Jimmy Jackson, had been found at an isolated farmhouse somewhere between Downham Market and Wisbech.

The call was referred to as a likely suicide, so the detective decides there is no need to hurry and disturb the relative peace of the countryside by putting on his siren and lights. He is listening to Radio 2, trying to answer the questions being posted on Ken Bruce's *Pop Master Quiz*. He is pleased with himself when he beats the winner by a massive nine points. Scoring a total of 30 out of 39 is no mean feat and it isn't for the first time that he wonders whether he shouldn't enter the contest himself. After all, he regularly scores more than the actual participants, so why not? There is of course the fear that if he actually took part, his brain might go soggy and he would end up with no points at all and become the laughing stock of the station.

After turning left over the bridge at Nordelph, the road straightens out into the distance. The seemingly endless fields on either side are showing the vibrant yellow of oil seed rape and the monotone green from recently emerging potato plants. About a mile and a half further, he turns left again and enters a farmyard with the main house standing back from the farm buildings. He takes a moment to survey the scene.

An ambulance sits outside a relatively new grain store. A visibly upset man in his thirties is pacing on his phone in front of the large barn doors. Two paramedics are talking to some other men who, by the look of their clothing, are most likely farmworkers.

DCI Culverhouse parks his car and walks towards

the assembled group of people. He introduces himself but before entering the building, signals to the ambulance crew to follow him to the side so he can have a private conversation. He has met one of the paramedics, Sally Carter, before so he turns to her first. She explains that they were called about fifty minutes earlier while they were driving back from delivering a cyclist with a suspected broken leg to the A&E department at the Queen Elizabeth Hospital in King's Lynn. On arrival at the farm, they were met by the two employees who showed them the body. As it was clear there was nothing they could do they moved outside to wait for the police. She informs the detective that the man on the phone is Jack Jackson, Jimmy's son, who had arrived a couple of minutes after them. Apparently he lived only a few houses further up the road and had seen the ambulance turn into the farm drive.

Culverhouse walks towards the three men and asks them to stay where they are as he would like to talk to them later. Jack Jackson is about to ask a question but before he can do so, Sally opens the barn door and the detective steps inside. He takes one look, turns to Sally and asks:

'Did his son see this?'

She nods.

'No wonder he is shaken.'

The second paramedic, Brian, suggests going outside to look after Jack.

What they are looking at is a man lying on his back in a pool of blood concentrated around the upper half of his body. He is wearing wellies, blue overalls and most of his body appears undamaged, apart from his head, which has lost any resemblance to what you would expect to see when looking at a human face. In fact there is no face at all, its front having been shot to pieces, no doubt the result of the fire power wielded by the 12 bore shotgun lying to the right of the body.

DCI Culverhouse takes a moment longer to take in the scene, choking down the bile rising from his stomach, as he surveys the gruesome remains. What would drive someone to do this to themselves?
He takes a deep breath before asking:

'And this is how you found him?'
Again Sally nods.

'Did you touch the body?'

'Yes. When we first came in Brian went over and spent a few minutes feeling his pulse and listening for a heartbeat but to no avail.'
It is clear, however, that Jimmy Jackson is dead - killing himself with his own shotgun.

Steve steps outside into the now bright sunlight of the beautiful spring morning, the fresh air

4

suppressing his rising nausea and unease. He walks to his car, rings into the station and summons the SOCO team from Norfolk police. Based in King's Lynn, these specialist scene of crime officers will probably take another half an hour or so, plenty of time for him to secure the barn door with police tape and talk to the three men, all of whom are looking at him expectantly. But before he does so he makes another call and asks for a doctor to be arranged.

'Why would he take his own life?' Jack Jackson asks. 'Why would he do this to me, Marion and the children?'

'It must be a terrible shock,' Steve replies. 'I presume Marion is your wife; have you spoken to her?'

Jackson nods.

'I gave her a ring. She teaches in Friday Bridge and is on her way. She is distraught.'

'I suggest you go straight home when she arrives. There's nothing you can do here and I'm sure you need some time together. Are the children at home?'

'At school. I presume we must go and collect them.'

At this moment, a black Audi A3 arrives. Jack Jackson starts sobbing while he embraces his crying wife. Steve feels bad interrupting them but says:

'I will come and visit you later today. In the

5

meantime, can I ask you not to contact anyone other than immediate family and not post anything on social media for the time being?'

They both nod but Steve wonders how much they've actually taken in.

When the Audi has left Steve walks over to the two farm hands. The taller one of the two replies his name is Jan Kowalski while the other man introduces himself as Viktor Nowak. They both work for Mr Jackson and live in a static caravan in nearby Salters Lode. Mr Kowalski explains they got up around seven o'clock. They would normally meet Mr Jackson in the yard at around eight. When he didn't turn up they thought nothing of it as this wasn't an unusual occurrence. After waiting a few minutes, they decided they might as well get on and started cleaning the crop sprayer, ready for use later in the day. Around nine o'clock Mr Nowak had walked to the house to collect the keys for the barn door and the tractor, which he found in their usual place in the lean-to by the back door. He had listened for a while to see if he could hear Mr Jackson get up but when all stayed quiet, he went back, and together with his colleague opened the grain store and found the body, lying in front of the new John Deere tractor. It was Mr Kowalski who immediately called 999.

A black Range Rover arrives and parks next to the

ambulance. A small man in a grey suit identifies himself as Doctor Walker and states the deceased is most likely one of his patients. He is given a pair of protective overshoes and gloves and makes his way inside the barn. As expected, he takes less than a few minutes to pronounce Mr Jackson dead. He appears quite shaken.

'I don't understand it,' he says. 'Why would he do something like this? He was always positive and enjoyed life. He was in excellent health as far as I remember. As a matter of fact, I have not seen him in the surgery for more than three years. The last time he made an appointment was around the time his wife died and he came in to ask for some sleeping tablets as he had trouble getting enough rest at night. I remember putting him on a repeat prescription and noticing he only used this service for a few months.'

'Do you have any knowledge whether he had any particular money worries or other concerns?'

'Like I said, I haven't seen him for years. As far as money worries go, I have no idea but I've never met a farmer who is not worried about money. I do remember hearing on the grapevine he'd suffered a substantial loss last year on his potato crop. And there was, of course, the theft of his tractor. But whether these things are relevant, I leave for others to decide.'

Steve thanks the doctor, gives him his card, and asks him to ring if he remembers anything else that might be significant.

When the SOCO officers arrive, Steve tells the officer in charge what he has found out so far, after which the team quickly and efficiently take over proceedings. He waits for a few minutes, enjoying the smells of the farmyard aroma he remembers so well from his childhood, before returning to the barn where both the doors have been opened to let the light in.

A tent is being erected around the body. One of the team is taking photographs while another is circling pieces of evidence, such as the remains of the farmer's cap, which is lying about three feet away between the body and the tractor. Two others are busying themselves with tape measures, no doubt charting the trajectory of the pellets. Steve, who by now has donned gloves and overshoes, notices the tractor is covered in small specks of blood and other materials, no doubt pieces of flesh carried from the impact of the shot.

Not long after the team are finished with the initial investigation, the customary anonymous black van arrives to take the body away to the mortuary. They proceed with a further detailed search of the barn and the rest of the yard before entering the farmhouse with the key supplied by Jack Jackson.

~

'So what happened in Nordelph?'

The question is asked by a tall woman in a black business suit. Her no-nonsense attitude is reflected in her style - comfortable but fashionable shoes, a simple ponytail framing her angular face with only a touch of make-up completing her appearance. This is Sarah Sutton, the formidable, yet passionate Detective Chief Superintendent of the Special Fenland Police Force. Her reputation for not taking any bullshit has earned her the nickname SS. But never to her face. Steve and his team aren't fools.

He quickly relates the events at the grain store and the suspected suicide.

'It shouldn't take too much of our time, I suppose,' DCS Sutton answers.

'I'm not really sure. Something's not quite right.'

'What do you mean?'

Steve waits a moment before speaking.

'Things don't add up,' he eventually replies. 'There is the immediate and fairly obvious issue of the position of the gun. I am not an expert but when talking to Jack Jackson this morning, I noticed he was left-handed. When I remarked on this, he told me it ran in the family and his son and father were the same. We'll need expert opinion on this of course but even with my limited experience, I think that if a left-handed person had fired the shot, the most likely direction the rifle would have fallen was either on the chest or to the left of the body. But it was lying nearly three feet away to the right. In addition, the reaction from the family was one of total surprise.'

DCS Sutton interrupts:

'Isn't it quite normal that people close to those with mental health issues or suicidal thoughts are often totally unaware of the struggles a friend or family member might be going through?'

'Fair point,' concedes Steve, 'but the doctor and the farmworkers all said the same thing. Mr Jackson had shown no signs of depression. I am planning to meet with a representative of the National Farmers' Union who apparently is an expert on these matters and might be able to fill me in on the extent other factors may have played their part, such as the stolen tractor and the bad potato harvest.'

'I see what you mean,' DCS Sutton responds. 'You better do some digging. Keep me informed and remember not to let on to the family that there is a tiny chance that all is not what it seems.'

2

Downham Market Police station had been downgraded a few years before from an active station to information point status only, with a civilian managing the enquiry desk during the day between the hours of nine and five. It was an ideal base, therefore, to house the Special Fenland Police Force which was established to deal with the increased criminal activity in the countryside.

The case of Tony Martin, a farmer who shot dead a burglar, had gained national notoriety. It had also revealed some of the weaknesses in having police forces confined to county boundaries. In response, the SFPF was formed and staffed with officers from Norfolk, Cambridgeshire and Lincolnshire covering the area commonly referred to as the Fens.

Most of the crimes they dealt with were farming related. Enforcing strict rules on the movement of livestock, illegal workers and lately, more frequently, the theft of heavy farm machinery. It adopted a multi-agency approach with active Home Office liaison to help with immigration issues, the National Farmers' Union with rural crime and community workers to deal with some of the more unpleasant fallout of the Brexit process in terms of hate crimes and suchlike.

When Steve had seen the post of Detective Chief Inspector advertised while he was working down in London for the Metropolitan Police, he had no hesitation in applying. He grew up in the Fens, his father was a farmer, and although he never had the desire to follow in his footsteps, he always hoped to return to the place of his birth one day. His application had been successful but it was not without personal cost. Of course, Julia, London born and bred, and his two sons had come with him but she never felt at home here.

It had not been long before cracks in their relationship started to appear and when Julia was offered her old job back in London, she was only too happy to accept. The boys had gone back with her to attend their old school and sometimes Steve felt like a divorced father with access rights only once a month. Of course, he could have gone back to London himself, but something prevented him from doing so. Was it the job which he thoroughly enjoyed, was it being back in the countryside where he grew up or was it something deeper? Had the cracks between him and Julia which appeared after moving here been there all along?

He didn't know and most of the time refused to let his mind be drawn into it. He soon found hard work during the day and a bottle of whiskey at night, while listening to Tom Waits, were the perfect remedies to keep any negative thoughts at bay.

As Steve was the second person to be appointed, after DCS Sutton, he played a full part in setting up the new taskforce. It had been agreed the team should reflect that three different police forces were involved and each would bring specialist and complementary skills.

One problem immediately apparent was the enormous area they needed to cover. It was nearly impossible for a detective from Lincoln to join the team in Downham Market as this would involve nearly five hours' travel each day.

In some ways, Steve thought, it would have been better to site the team more centrally, in Peterborough or Spalding perhaps, but it was simply a case of cost and the empty Downham Market station was by far the cheapest option.

In the end, the team assembled were, apart from DCS Sutton and Steve, Detective Inspector John

Baker from Norfolk, Detective Inspector Katia Starling from Cambridgeshire and Detective Inspector Simon Woods from Lincolnshire. Woods lived in Sutton Bridge, not far from the Norfolk/Lincolnshire shire border. In addition, there was Sergeant Dave Newman and a civilian, Magdalena Bowen, or Maddie, as she preferred to be called, who staffed the enquiry desk. There were no uniformed officers permanently attached but each force had identified a number of police constables who could step in when needed and also take part in any specialised training.

~

After talking to DCS Sutton, Steve grabs a quick sandwich before inviting Sergeant Newman to accompany him on his visit to Jack Jackson and his wife. When they arrive it is obvious from their demeanour that both are in shock. Steve decides the best thing is to let them talk, only occasionally asking a few questions. If necessary, a formal interview can be arranged at a later stage. Jack again asks why his father would do such a thing.

'That is what we are trying to find out,' Steve replies, 'and the more information you can give us, the sooner we'll have an answer.'

This seems to focus Jack.

'We knew dad had some problems but we never guessed how desperate he must have felt. We all felt bad when mum died but we had known for years it was only a matter of time, as the cancer she was suffering from was incurable. All we could see was how well he bounced back after the funeral. He enjoyed work and started taking more of an interest in the boys, regularly taking them to Carrow Road to see their favourite football team, Norwich City.'

'Not only that,' Marion added, 'he lately was talking about maybe finding a female companion, someone to have the occasional meal with or spending a day down at Welney bird watching.'

'Did he find someone?'

'We think he did,' answers Jack, 'but we never met her. He was a bit secretive about it. But he has twice missed Sunday dinner, which he has never done before!'

'What about the stolen tractor? How did he take that?'

'Better than I expected. It was only two years old and very expensive but we were pleased he bought it because it meant he was looking forward to the future. When it got stolen, he was a bit upset but in the end, it was more of an inconvenience rather than a disaster because the insurance company paid out quickly and so he was able to replace it almost immediately.'

'And the potato harvest?'

Steve had been wondering about this as he knew from his own dad the crop that year had been excellent.

'Yes,' answered Jack. 'He was screwed over well and good on that one.'

'How so?'

'He has been dealing with the same supermarket chain for over ten years. Selling his crop in advance at an agreed price. But because last year was a bumper crop, the supermarket was able to buy the potatoes cheaper on the open market. And although they signed a contract, they got out of it by claiming our potatoes were too big for their packing machines. As a result, he lost nearly £15,000.00. Dad contacted the NFU but, although they were sympathetic, there was nothing they could do.'

'How did your father take it?'

'He was annoyed and angry but I wouldn't say it made him depressed or anything like that.'

'Could he cope with such a loss?'

'I would say so. Marion does his books for him and

the potatoes represented only a fifth of his income. In the end, he was able to sell most on the open market anyway, so the final loss was probably half of what it first looked like.'

'Are you suggesting he had no money worries?'

'We don't think so. When mum died, we had a meeting and everything was okay. He was running a £50,000.00 overdraft facility with the bank but the mortgage on the farm was paid off. He also had two ISAs each with £20,000.00 in them, which he had earmarked for our boys' education. And his savings account had well over £100,000.00 in it.'

Steve thanks them, thinking maybe he should talk to his own dad to see how he is doing and make sure he is alright. He says his goodbyes, leaves his card and promises he will keep them informed. He does not share his suspicion their father's death might not have been suicide.

After driving away from the Jackson's house Steve and Sergeant Newman make for the local Fenland NFU office. They have phoned ahead and are met by Charlie Goodyear, a stocky man with what best can be described as a jolly face. After he introduces himself, he refers to Jimmy's death as 'Tragic, yet another one,' but in spite of the sombre words, Steve notices his facial expression does not change.

'What do you mean? *Yet another one.*'

'Jimmy's suicide is the third on my patch in the last two years. And I must say, I didn't see this one coming. I knew he had some bad times with the potatoes, the tractor and his wife dying but he seemed perfectly upbeat to me. Mind you,' he seemed to remind himself, 'you don't always recognise the signs, do you?'

'When did you last see him?'

'Officially after the business with the potatoes and also with the tractor. We couldn't help him with the potatoes but his tractor was insured through NFU Mutual and we pride ourselves on settling these claims very quickly so the work, especially at harvest time, does not get interrupted too much.'

'What did you mean when you said *officially, Steve* asks?

'I meant as part of my work but,' he smiles conspiratorially, 'I also saw him a few weeks ago in the Carpenters' Arms in Denver. He didn't see me because he had his back to me while sitting in a corner having a meal with his lady friend.'

'You don't happen to know her name, do you?'

'I'm afraid I don't, but I remember saying to the missus, Jimmy's obviously over his wife's death seeing he's spending his Sunday evening with a woman half his age.'

'Could you describe this woman to me?'

'Oh yes. Stunning she was. I couldn't keep my eyes off her. Long dark hair tied back flat against her head, nice make-up and smart clothes which fitted perfectly. You know, a little tight, like the foreign women around here dress.' He winked at the detectives when he said this. Steve did not respond but instead gave him his card and finished the conversation by saying, 'If you do remember anything else, could you give me a ring? Oh, and when did you see him in the pub?'

'Let me see - that would not have been last Sunday but the Sunday before.'

3

Although it is now nearly five o'clock, Steve assembles the team in the incident room. He has put up a map of the area, some of the photos supplied by the SOCO team and a number of questions, the two most important in capital letters:

SUICIDE? - MURDER?

Apart from Steve, the three detectives and Sergeant Newman are seated around a big table in front of the evidence wall. He is about to start when DCS Sutton appears and sits down. It is at this moment Maddie enters the room.

'Sorry to interrupt,' she says, 'but I think one of you better come down. I've got a hysterical woman downstairs who says her cousin has been murdered.'

DI Kate Starling goes downstairs with Maddie, where she finds a young lady pacing the foyer. She is visibly distraught. Her make-up has run down her cheeks and she is in floods of tears. The detective leads her into the small downstairs interview room while Maddie, without asking, moves to the kitchen to make her a cup of tea. When asked to tell what has happened, Lena Tobinska, as she introduces herself, explains in almost perfect English that, after her day shift at the canning factory in Wisbech, she returned to the mobile home she shares with her cousin Alecja in the village of Salters Lode only to find her cousin gone, but with the kitchen and living area covered in blood. She had panicked and driven straight to the police station on her moped.

'So you didn't actually see her?' DI Starling says gently. 'Why do you think she is dead? Might she have had an accident and got herself to the hospital?' Whilst saying this Starling makes a mental note to immediately ring the two nearest hospitals to ask about A&E admissions.

Lena starts crying again.

'She is dead! She was warned if she did not do as they told her, she would be killed.'

'Who told her that?'

'I don't know his name,' she answers 'but he comes to our house and collects the rent and a couple of weeks ago he said that if Alecja did not pay what she owed him, he would kill her.'

DI Starling asks Maddie, who by now has made

the tea, to sit with Lena while she returns upstairs where the others look at her expectantly when she walks into the room and explains what she has been told.

Before long DI Starling, DI Baker and Lena are on their way to Salters Lode and Maddie is ringing the hospitals. Those left behind try to concentrate on the original purpose of their meeting but find it difficult to do so.

As Sergeant Newman puts it:

'So now we possibly have two murders in one day.'

'Not only that,' says Steve, 'two murders and only five miles between them.'

'Let's not jump to conclusions. We need to stick to the facts,' DCS Sutton replies. 'From where I'm standing we are more likely have a suicide and a missing person who may or may not be injured.'

She is correct of course, Steve thinks, but he feels in his guts something isn't quite right.

Salters Lode is only three miles from Downham Market; the two detectives and Lena soon arrive at the mobile home, which is part of a small complex of similar structures, six in total. The caravan park is about half a mile down a concrete track and invisible from the road as it is situated behind some abandoned farm buildings. Such sites have become a common feature in the Fen landscape during the last ten years and are mainly used to house many of the thousands of Eastern European farmworkers. Although often in bad condition, the private landlords and gangmasters who operate them have no problem letting them at extraordinary high rents to willing workers, desperate to find somewhere to live.

DI Starling asks Lena to wait in the car. She and DI Baker walk to the door, knock, and when there is no reply open it without actually going inside. DI Starling turns to her colleague who nods. Lena has not exaggerated. There is blood everywhere and whoever's blood it is will surely be in a poor state by now. Both detectives return to the car and put on their protective clothing. They go back inside the caravan, carefully making sure not to disturb anything as it is obvious some kind of struggle has taken place. A chair is lying on its side, a cup and some glasses are shattered on the floor. After making sure there is no one inside, the detectives leave, sealing the door with police tape and informing Steve back at the station. He tells them there have been no admissions of a person corresponding with Alecja's description in either of the local hospitals. Steve next informs the SOCO team and, with DCS Sutton's approval, requests the release to the unit of the three constables earmarked by Norfolk Police.

Back at the site, DI Starling sits in the car with Lena while DI Baker takes a closer look at the other mobile homes. Strange, he thinks, if this was a street anywhere else, neighbours by now would have gathered and asked questions. Here, however, no one appears to be curious. Some people are clearly in as he can see television lights flickering in at least three of the other mobile homes. He decides to wait until back-up arrives and walks around the old farm buildings to have a cigarette, out of sight of DI Starling, who disapproves of smoking, especially when on duty.

When he turns a corner, around what once must have been an old chicken shed, DI Baker notices two men walking away.

'Excuse me,' he calls. The men stop and turn towards him.

'What you want?' the first man asks in broken English.

'Do you live here?' John asks. The man nods towards the mobile homes.

'We want no trouble. You police?'
John introduces himself. 'You're not in trouble,' he says.
The first man gives a tired laugh.

'With police, we always in trouble.'

John sighs. It is true, in spite of all the cross-community initiatives, many of the immigrants have a deep mistrust of the police. Sometimes this has to do with their experiences back home but more often than not it is the result of insensitive responses from local officers. One policeman had even thought it was acceptable to display a prominent English Defence League sticker on the back window of his car, which was parked in full view of the police station in Wisbech. Sadly, DI Baker realises no amount of diversity courses will ever shift the mindset of some of his colleagues.

He offers both men a cigarette, which they accept. Not for the first time, DI Baker notices how a simple act like sharing a cigarette puts people at ease.

'Did you see anything unusual today?'

'What you mean?' replies the man in a much friendlier tone.

'Any strangers or cars you've not seen before visiting the home of the two women?'

'We've seen nothing. We've only just got back from work.'

While DI Baker is questioning the two men, DI Starling has been talking, or rather listening, to Lena Tobinska. Much of the stuff Lena is telling her is probably irrelevant and resulting from the emotional state she is in, but experience has taught her if you let people talk, something might come up, which could shine further light on a situation. Lena, in between sobs, told her she and her cousin have been in the country for two years and at first were doing well. They found work quickly, through a job agency in Wisbech, first on the land and later in the canning factory which they preferred as it was dry and gave a regular income.

But about six months ago, Alecja had a fallout with a chargehand at the factory. In the argument, which centred on her cousin looking at her mobile phone while at work, the man became aggressive and pushed her while trying to take her phone off her. Alecja slapped him and called him a *"Skurwysyn"* which Lena explains is a Polish insult, like calling someone "a son of a bitch". As a result, she was sacked on the spot. As they couldn't pay the rent on only one wage, they were threatened with eviction from their room in Wisbech.

Alecja went back to the agency, which put her in touch with Mick Mendham, a local gangmaster. Big Mick, as he was known, soon found her a job on one of the local farms and she returned to working on the land. He also offered the cousins the mobile home they now lived in. Rent was payable weekly in cash with no receipt given. All had been fine for a while but when the farm she worked on had a bad potato harvest, Alecja once again was made redundant without receiving the back pay she was owed.

After losing her second job, Alecja had fallen behind on the rent. Before long, she owed Mick a sizeable sum.

Then one day, out of the blue, Mick came by and told them he had sold the mobile home and from now on, they had to pay the rent to the new owner, another gangmaster, whose name she didn't know.

'Can you describe him?'

'He's a big man who speaks English with some kind of accent. Alecja asked him for work but he said he wouldn't employ her as he'd heard she was trouble. And he would make sure none of the other agencies would touch her either. It was unfair because there were plenty of jobs but this guy was hell-bent on preventing her from working.'

'Any idea why?'

'My cousin is very beautiful. I think he wanted her to get into debt so in the end she would be forced to work for him in his brothel in Peterborough. I paid off part of what she owes him, after which he stopped pressuring Alecja for a while, but I don't have enough savings to pay off everything. It got a bit better after he employed another man to collect the rent. He is good and always talks to me and never mentions my cousin. But every now and then, the big guy comes himself and argues with Alecja.'

'Why didn't you simply leave and move elsewhere or go back home?'

'How can we move back home with no money and no passport?' Lena cries.

'No passport?'

'Part of being allowed to stay in the home after Mick sold it was to give our passports to the new landlord as security,' she replies, sobbing quietly now.

This is modern-day slavery! DI Starling realises, but for now they would have to concentrate on finding Alecja. At this moment, DI Baker knocks on the car window, pointing to the SOCO van and two patrol cars coming down the concrete track.

~

Back at the station, Steve is thinking about the interviews he conducted with the family and the National Farmers' Union representative. DCS Sutton, DI Woods and he stayed together for about twenty minutes after their colleagues left for Salters Lode before DCS Sutton decided the best course of action was to contact the other forces, put out a missing person alert and suggest reconvening first thing in the morning. Steve has stayed behind to get an update from DI Starling and her colleague. But when they return, they have little to report other than that Ms Tobinska had not exaggerated and something is definitely amiss. But there doesn't seem to be much they can do right now, so they decide to wait until the morning when the SOCO team might have some more news.

Steve doesn't have to wait that long. One of the scene of crime officers rings to tell him that they have found a trail of blood leading from the caravan to the parking area, where it stops. They have not been able to find an imprint of tyre marks on the smooth concrete. Even so, they have decided a detailed search of the surrounding area is not necessary as they are convinced the injured person has left in a vehicle. Steve thanks his colleague, gets in his car, and drives home. He feels uneasy. Surely there is more they should be doing. But however hard he tries, he can't think of anything.

TUESDAY

4

When Steve walks into the incident room the next morning at eight, most of the others are already there. They are soon joined by the three extra police officers assigned to the case. Steve is immediately struck by the presence of PC Eva Lappinska. Her parents moved to Britain from Poland and brought her up speaking English, Polish and Russian. It is partly for these skills that she has been assigned to the Fenland Force. She is also active in community engagement projects and often gives up her spare time to act as an interpreter for the substantial Polish community in the Fens. Steve has worked with her before and likes her. Apart from her language skills, she is an excellent officer all round and often goes the extra mile.

'I think we're all here,' DCS Sutton says. 'In a minute, I will ask DCI Culverhouse and DI Starling to update us on the latest developments, but for now I want to make it clear that so far, we have no conclusive proof we are dealing with two murders. Can I ask you all to be careful in what we say during interviews and door-to-door enquiries? The last thing we want is panic in the community.'

She moves away from the head of the table and takes a chair at the back.

DI Starling stands up and explains what they found at the caravan and also relates some of her conversation with Lena.

'I think we need to talk to her again,' she says. 'She was open about most things but I'm not sure she was totally truthful about not knowing some of the names of the people who made her cousin's life a misery. I don't think she is lying, more that she is afraid. Also, she mentioned a brothel in Peterborough as well as telling me both cousins were made to give up their passports as security and are therefore trapped. Something we might be interested in following up later.'

After she has given the rest of the room all the relevant points, DCS Sutton interrupts and asks if there are any questions.

'Where is she now?' DI Woods asks.

31

'I took her to a friend in King's Lynn. I told her we would contact her again this morning and ring her if or when we have any news.'

'What I don't get,' PC Lappinska says, 'is why she drove to the police station rather than ringing 999. Or went to one of the other caravans to ask for help.'

'Good point,' replies DCS Sutton, looking expectantly at DI Starling.

Slightly embarrassed, she replies:

'I didn't think of asking. I felt letting her talk was the best course of action.'

'No worries, we can ask her later. DI Baker, you were there; anything to add?'

John Baker stirs his coffee.

'Not really, but I did briefly speak to two men from the other caravans who said they had been at work all day and hadn't seen anything. I was interrupted when the SOCO team arrived, so I had no chance to follow it up.'

'Thanks,' Steve says, 'it is definitely a line of enquiry we have to explore further and of course, we must try and find Mick Mendham as well as the mystery rent collector.'

After this, Steve briefly explains what he found out from speaking to Jimmy Jackson's son and daughter-in-law (very little) before recounting his visit to Charlie Goodyear at the NFU offices.

'Let's break for coffee,' DCS Sutton suggests, 'and meet back here in fifteen minutes. DCI Culverhouse, can you join me in my office, please?'

One of the best things about meetings in DCS Sutton's office, Steve thinks, is that she has installed a state-of-the-art expresso machine and the coffee is always excellent. Once they both have their cups and are sitting down, Sarah turns to Steve.

'What do you think?'

'Frankly, we haven't got much to go on but the disappearance of Alecja bothers me the most at this moment in time. Someone doesn't simply disappear around here, especially not in such a small community as the European workers. I would like us to put all our efforts into trying to find her as quickly as possible.'

DCS Sutton nods encouragingly.

'I suggest DI Starling and PC Baker continue interviewing Lena as a matter of urgency. I'd like to get DI Woods to start searching for Mick Mendham by visiting the employment agencies in Wisbech. It might also be useful to find out what the score is with current employment demand and get a feel of what's possibly going on. He can take one of the PCs, Pete Redding, with him.'

'I would like to visit the caravan site in Nordelph

and see the setup for myself. I'll take Eva with me; she will be useful when it comes to talking to some of the people in the caravans. In the meantime, Sergeant Newman and,' he paused while checking his notes, 'PC Sheldon, can stay here and concentrate on locating contact details for Mick Mendham as well as doing a search on social media on the two cousins and anyone else associated with them.'

'Sounds good,' Sarah replies. 'What about the other matter with the suicide? Have you established any links between the two incidents?'

Was it his imagination or did she sound a touch ironic, Steve wonders?

'I think,' he says, ignoring the last question, 'we'd better wait for the pathologist's report.'

'I agree,' replies his boss, after which they make their way back to the meeting room and explain the plan of action to the others. Everybody gets up quickly, keen to get on.

'Back here at four.' Steve says before walking to his own car with Eva and heading out to Salters Lode.

5

*Around the time Steve is talking to DCS Sutton,
Alecja wakes up. She is lying in a bed but it is not
her own. Where is she? She tries to sit up but the
moment she puts her hands on the mattress to lift
herself up, she lets out a sharp yelp caused by pain
shooting through her arms. She realises she's
actually been sleeping on a settee. What has
happened? She lies down again and tries to think.
Suddenly the horror of it all comes back to her, the
knock on the door, then a big man standing there
with a smile on his face, telling her to get ready, they
are going for a ride. Her response, telling him to
fuck off, and him pushing her while she grabs a
chair, trying to defend herself. She remembers
ending up on the floor with the man sitting on top of
her while another man crouches down next to her.
He is wearing a balaclava, so she can't see his face.
She recalls him talking to her gently, saying, 'Go on
love, you don't want all this trouble. Tell us where*

Jimmy has stashed the money.' It slowly comes back to her, of course, the money. Jimmy had rung her the night before and told her he had received some unexpected money and was hoping to see her today so he could pay her the wages she'd lost when he sacked her. She remembers playfully arguing with him and telling him it wasn't necessary. She also knew she had to accept it, not only because she needed the money and had earned it, but also because it would make Jimmy feel less guilty about sacking her. And how she told the man sitting next to her to fuck off and that she had no idea about Jimmy's money and how he had produced a syringe and injected it in her thigh in spite of her trying as hard as she could to wriggle free. And how then everything had gone dark.

And now, the same sensation engulfs her: it is as if all this thinking has totally worn her out. Before long she drifts back into a deep, dreamless sleep.

6

After explaining to Eva that they are just going to have a look at the caravan site where the two women live, Steve relaxes and lets his mind wonder. Were there any links between the two cases? Not really, but there are a number of coincidences. Both incidents happened within five miles from each other. Both incidents most likely occurred on the same day. Where that might be common in a big city, it was definitely not normal in the countryside. Also, it was very likely that the farm from which Alecja Tobinska was sacked after the bad potato harvest was Jimmy Jackson's. If that was the case, it would mean that Jimmy, Mick Mendham and Alecja all knew each other! Finally, Jimmy had been seen with a mystery Eastern European woman only a week and a bit before he died and Alecja disappeared. His thoughts are interrupted when Eva points towards a road on the right. Steve indicates, slows down, and turns onto the concrete track leading to the caravan park.

While Steve and Eva are busying themselves in Salters Lode, DI Starling and DI Baker are making their way to King's Lynn. After the usual hold-up at the Hardwick Roundabout, John Baker, who is driving, turns onto the bypass, which circles the town on the eastern side and is the main road to Sandringham, Hunstanton and the North Norfolk Coast. As a result, it is often blocked with holiday traffic, especially caravans. However, this being mid-morning on a weekday in the spring, the traffic isn't too bad.

At the hospital roundabout, John turns left and almost immediately left again. They follow the road for about a mile through a 1960s housing estate before turning onto a stretch of newly built dual carriageway, which leads to a brand new housing development. The house Lena is staying in is a small, two-storey property with a tiny front garden surrounded by a newly erected picket fence. Both detectives notice all the curtains are closed. When they ring the bell, there is no immediate answer but DI Baker observes the tiniest twitching of the curtains at one of the two upstairs windows. After ringing the bell for the second time, DI Starling gets her phone out and rings Lena's mobile. She answers on the seventh ring. DI Starling explains they are at the front door.

'Sorry,' Lena replies, 'I am no longer there.'

'But we need to speak.'

'Do you know the café in the Walks?' Lena asks. 'I can meet you there in twenty minutes.'

It will have to do, DI Starling thinks, not at all happy with the way things have gone so far. *She* is supposed to be in charge of proceedings, not Lena. Not for the first time, she feels she sometimes is treated with less respect than her male counterparts. Is it something in her personality? Is it because she has only recently been promoted or is it simply because she is a woman? Whatever it is, she thinks, they are wasting valuable time.

At the same time as DI Starling and DI Baker are making their way to the Walks, DI Woods and PC Redding are driving along the narrow and twisting road to Wisbech, beside the Well Creek. Although it feels like a minor road, it is nevertheless busy with lorries and trucks, many with foreign number plates. In fact, this road is the shortest route from the North Sea ports of Harwich and Felixstowe to the agricultural and food industries located in Wisbech and Peterborough. 'I suggest,' DI Woods says to his colleague, 'we start with another cup of coffee in the square and formulate a plan for the day.' Pete Redding smiles to himself. It is well known DI Woods likes to start every day and every investigation with coffee, a cigarette and a large slice of cake. How the man is not fat, no one at the station can explain. But it is not a bad idea, Pete thinks, and he suggests: 'We could use the time to check for job vacancies and the names of employment agencies. It should give us some idea of where to start.'

'Excellent idea,' DI Woods replies. 'I can see you and I will get on well together.' With this, he turns into a car park in the middle of town and parks in a space not far from the Wisbech Museum.

Any anger or frustration DI Starling might have felt towards Lena disappears the moment she sets eyes on the pathetic sad creature waiting for her next to the children's playground opposite the café. She has obviously been crying and no amount of make-up can hide the shadows under her eyes due to lack of sleep. DI Starling's first instinct is to put her arms around her but she holds back, remembering the tutor in her psychology class at university telling them the last thing people in an emotional fragile state need is others piling more emotion onto them.

A calm and structured approach is often more

40

beneficial. So instead, she leads Lena to a table outside, away from the ones near the children's playground, which are occupied mainly by mothers and the occasional father, keeping an eye on their offspring while enjoying a coffee and a chat.

DI Baker offers to get some drinks, a cappuccino for himself and expressos for the two women. Immediately Lena turns to DI Starling,

'Tell me, have you come to bring me bad news? Is Alecja dead? Please tell me.'

'No,' DI Starling replies. 'I have no bad news but no good news either. Everything is as it was yesterday, I'm afraid. It is why I'm here: you and I need to have a proper talk and find out if there is anything you can tell me that might help us find Alecja.'

She realises she sounds quite firm but notices Lena relaxes ever so slightly.

DI Baker returns with the coffees and for a moment they are all quiet. DI Starling next explains there have been no sightings, no response to the missing person request and no admissions to a hospital anywhere in the region. At this point, Lena starts sobbing quietly.

'She is dead,' she whispers, 'I can feel it deep inside; we are like sisters. I feel what she feels.'

'We don't know that yet,' DI Starling replies. 'What

we need to do now is to start at the beginning and find out as much as we can. Don't leave anything out because you think it is not important. We need to get a full picture of what has happened over the last twenty-four hours but anything else you can remember from the last six months since Alecja was sacked from the canning factory might also be relevant. Inspector Baker will make notes but if it's alright with you, I would also like to record our conversation.'

Lena nods and DI Starling puts her phone on the table, pressing the record button.

'Let's start with where we are now,' she suggests. 'Is everything alright between your friend and you? Is she still happy for you to stay at her house?'

'Oh yes, no problem,' Lena responds. 'The only reason I went out quite early is because my friend does shift work and needs to sleep in the day. I did not want to disturb her. Also, I needed some fresh air and do some shopping. I have nothing: all my stuff is in the caravan.'

DI Baker interjects,

'I will talk to Chief Inspector Culverhouse to see if we can retrieve some of your belongings.'

'But I don't want to go back there,' Lena exclaims, and she starts crying again.

'It's alright,' he replies, 'we can do it for you.'

'Back to the beginning,' DI Starling suggests. 'When was the last time you saw Alecja?'

'Yesterday morning,' Lena replies, 'before I set off for work, probably around seven.'

'And how was she?'

'Normal, a bit sleepy but she looked happy and sounded positive. I asked her why she was up so early and she told me she would tell me after I came back from work.'

'What about the last couple of weeks?' DI Baker asks. 'Maybe starting with the argument about the rent with... What was his name again?'

'I'm not sure but I've heard people call him Curly.' DI Starling smiles to herself: typical of John, using his reassuring tone, to get an answer out of her about the identity of the man. This after Lena had told them yesterday she had no idea of what his name was.

'Will you excuse me a minute?' she says, picking up her phone and sending a quick text to Steve and DI Woods, alerting them to the name Curly. She puts the phone back on the table, indicating to Lena to continue.

'Like I told you yesterday, this man Curly was putting pressure on Alecja because of the rent and also because she refused to work in the brothel in Peterborough. But, when I said we will pay what we can, please be patient, he lost it and said to me:

43

"You stay out of it. This is between me and her," pointing at Alecja.

"She has plenty of money but she doesn't want you to know about it; she could easily pay all the rent if she wanted to."

She is shaking visibly now, so DI Starling leans over and puts her hand on Lena's. Lena takes a deep breath and continues:

'He turned directly to Alecja and said:

"You think I don't know about your little scheme with your fancy man. This is your last chance. You have the money. Pay up or else!"

'At this point, he slid his forefinger across his throat and told me:

"You have a week to sort this!"

'He then left, slamming the door behind him.'

While recalling the story, Lena becomes more and more upset.

'What do you think it all means?' DI Starling asks gently.

'I thought he was just threatening like he did before but now I'm not sure anymore.' She starts crying again and DI Starling notices several of the other customers looking at them. She turns to DI Baker, who nods.

'I think, Lena, the best we can do now is to take you back to the station where we can talk without

44

interruptions. I promise I'll drop you off at your friend's once we've finished.'

They get up and walk quietly back to their car through the Walks, along the beautiful central tree-lined avenue in the middle of this splendid Victorian park. Not that any of them take any of it in as they are all consumed by their own thoughts.

~

While the others disappear to their cars after the meeting, Sergeant Newman and PC Sheldon make their way to the computer room. This part of the building used to be the nerve centre of the police station when it was still operational. And in spite of the fact that most of the hardware has been removed, it still has the relevant IT infrastructure to support all the demands the small team might have in terms of technology. This includes direct access to the national crime computer database.

While Sergeant Newman goes to get them another coffee PC Sheldon sits down in front of his computer and sighs. He had hoped he would be chosen to do some real investigating but as per normal, he was asked to do the boring research bit back at the station. Once, when he had complained about this to

Sergeant Newman, the older man had laughed and said,

'That is what you get for doing a degree in computer studies.' Fair enough, I suppose, he thinks, but it rankles nevertheless.

But before long, both he and Sergeant Newman are fully engaged in their task. After only a few minutes, Ben Sheldon exclaims:

'Found it!' He points at the screen.

'Here's Mick Mendham's address as well as lots of other information, including a photo of him.'

'Amazing!' Sergeant Newman is impressed. 'How did you manage to get it so quickly?'

'Simple,' says Ben, 'I put his name in Google and a link appeared which took me straight to his website.'

'Well, I never expected him to have a website but this is great. Let's get the relevant details over to DI Woods immediately.'

At this moment, DCS Sutton walks into the room.

'Excellent work,' she says after Sergeant Newman explains this quick result to her.

'I would like you to go through all the information on the website to give us some idea of how he operates.'

She turns to Ben:

'PC Sheldon, can you concentrate on finding out more about Alecja Tobinska and her cousin, please.'

Sergeant Newman is relieved. Although he is reasonably competent with using computers, it does not come naturally. Reading information on a website is a task he is comfortable and happy with, but there is also something else. From briefly seeing Lena the day before, he presumes the cousins to be in their late 20s, exactly the same age as his own two daughters. He does not like the idea of prying into the private lives of young women, however relevant to the case this might be.

PC Sheldon, on the other hand, is soon in his element. He is fully aware he isn't allowed to illegally access any sites or files but it is amazing what you can do without breaking the law. It doesn't take him long to find Alecja's Facebook and Instagram pages and as he'd hoped, she has not put in any filters to restrict access. This means he can read all her public posts from the last couple of months. Already forgetting about his disappointment at being given this task, he settles in and attacks the job with relish.

7

Sarah Sutton is sitting in her office eating a chocolate biscuit and looking at the steam coming from her recently poured cappuccino. She feels uneasy. With her whole team - well most of them - out and about in the countryside doing things, she feels out of touch and distant from what is happening. She was warned this would happen by her previous boss and mentor, who told her that with promotion comes frustration and alienation because you are no longer engaged in working the coalface and your relationship with your colleagues inevitably changes. Or, as Randy Newman puts it, "It's lonely at the top."

It hasn't been all bad though. She likes and trusts her small team and feels her and Steve have a good working relationship. Of course, she knows the team gossip behind her back and she doesn't like her nickname, but she likes to think they also respect her in the same way she respects them. But she has never been one who easily makes friends or mixes socially. When she was a regular constable, she'd never been "one of the lads". She doesn't enjoy pubs, other than to go for lunch when out on a walk, maybe. She watches little telly, so doesn't know the celebrities or shows others are discussing during coffee and lunch breaks. In fact, no one from her small group of friends is in the police force. If she is honest, she is happiest when she is out running on her own on a nice summer's evening with the sun setting over the Fenland countryside.

But the unease she feels today is different: this is more to do with the actual case. It all feels disjointed. Yes, they are following several lines of enquiry but somehow, the sense of urgency felt yesterday has diminished. But what exactly gives her this uneasy feeling?

At this moment, her phone rings.

It is Maddy.

'I've got Alan Phelan from the *Fenland Gazette* on the phone for you. Shall I tell him you're in a meeting?'

She thinks about it for a minute and suddenly realises what is missing from the enquiry.

'No thanks, Maddy,' she replies, 'it's okay, put him through.'

Taking a sip of coffee, she replies to the caller's

'Good morning,' with a cheery 'Good morning to you too Alan, to what do I owe the pleasure?'

'Well,' the journalist replies, 'I've heard on the grapevine there is an internal police alert out for a missing person, a Polish girl. I thought you might like us to make some space in tomorrow's paper and give the disappearance some extra publicity.'

'You are too good, Alan,' Sarah laughs, 'and you'll do it without wanting any further information? Noble of you indeed.'

'Of course, some further information would be necessary for the story,' Alan responds. 'It is true then that you are in fact looking for a missing girl?'

'We are, but at this moment, I cannot give you any more details. But I promise once we have established whether or not we are dealing with a possible criminal disappearance or not, you will be one of the first to know. In the meantime, I would like you to keep this under your hat. The last thing we want is for the rumour mill to put two and two together and make five.'

'You do know there are rumours going around already, don't you? Father Connelly told me it was the only topic of conversation at the coffee morning in the Catholic Church in Wisbech today.'

'I'm sorry,' DCS Sutton says, 'we have a meeting

this afternoon. Give me a ring around six and I might have some more news for you. But only if you stay away from it until then. And I will monitor your website throughout the day,' she adds half-jokingly, half-seriously.

This is it, she thinks to herself after she puts the phone down, *this is what's been bothering me.* Normally when a person goes missing, there is all the excitement of public appeals and involvement from family, neighbours and complete strangers in trying to find the person concerned. What they were doing now was thorough and methodical but on a small scale. After seeing the photos of the caravan from where Alecja had disappeared, there is no doubt in her mind that the young woman is in imminent danger. They need to step it up.

She checks her watch: lunchtime. She gets her phone out and texts Steve to get back to the station as soon as he has finished in Salters Lode. Next, she contacts both the Norfolk County Police headquarters in Wymondham for more back-up as well as asking Cambridgeshire Police to release their three dedicated Fenland officers.

After this, she takes another biscuit though she knows she shouldn't if she wants to keep her figure. Never mind, she feels excited and she can always spend an extra half hour in the gym tonight. That should do it.

8

After parking the car, Steve and Eva first make for Lena and Alecja's mobile home. They find the scene much as described by DI Starling and John. Steve examines some of the photos supplied by the SOCO team and concludes nothing appears to have been disturbed.

Although his colleagues have gone through the place thoroughly, Steve puts on his protective clothing before he goes inside. He always likes to see things for himself and get a feel of the place. The two bedrooms look undisturbed. It is clear Lena and Alecja are extremely tidy people as both beds are made and clothes neatly folded. Steve can't remember when he last made his bed, probably when Julia and the boys came to visit.

Both bedrooms are more or less the same, each furnished with a double bed, a wardrobe and a small desk. Steve carefully checks the desk drawers but doesn't find anything of interest. Some jewellery, an

53

unused notepad and a packet of condoms. Something is missing, he realises, there is nothing personal here. No photos. No letters. Nothing to distinguish this place as someone's home.

He mentions this to Eva, who laughs.

'Welcome to the 21st century. People don't write letters anymore. All that stuff, especially photos, is kept on your mobile or tablet.'

Of course, Steve realises, that's why there are no laptops or computers in the caravan. But nothing else strikes him as suspicious and after resealing the door and re-applying the police tape, they make their way to the other homes on the site.

Like DI Baker the previous night, both Steve and Eva notice how quiet the site is. The whole place has an eerie deserted feel to it, especially as there are hardly any cars parked anywhere. After knocking on the first three doors without success, they have more luck at number four. A man in his thirties opens the door before they have a chance to knock and says:

'Can I help you?'

Before Steve can answer, he continues in reasonable English: 'You are the police, yes? I remember you from the farm yesterday. What has happened to the girls in the caravan?' He points at Lena's and Alecja's mobile home. Steve realises he is talking to Mr Kowalski, one of the farm workers he met yesterday.

'Can we come in, please?'

The man nods; Steve and Eva step inside. There they find a tidy kitchen and quite a spacious living room with a tatty armchair, settee, TV and a dining table with four chairs. One of the chairs is occupied by another man who Steve recognises as Mr Nowak. On the table are two bottles of beer and a pack of cards. Steve introduces Eva without giving her surname.

'Thank you,' Steve says on behalf of both Eva and himself when Mr Kowalski offers them a beer. It's a bit too early for us and we're working. How are you both? It must have been a terrible shock finding Mr Jackson.'

'It was,' Mr Kowalski answers. 'He was a good man and a good boss. But how can we help? We told you all we know yesterday.'

'Don't worry,' Steve replies. 'It is not why we are here. You asked about Lena and Alecja. How well do you know them?'

'Only a little bit, they have not lived here long and they do not speak to us much.'

Mr Nowak interrupts him and says something to him in Polish. When he's finished, Mr Kowalski turns to Steve and Eva,

'Viktor thinks they are a bit stuck-up, and the older one, I think her name is Lena, thinks she is too good for us. But he does like Alecja; in fact, we both do. We worked with her for Mr Jackson for a little while until the problem with the potatoes. But we haven't seen them for a few days. Why is there blue tape around their caravan? Are they alright?'

'That is what we are trying to find out,' says Steve. 'Lena is okay but we think Alecja may have been attacked yesterday. Did you see or hear anything?'

Mr Kowalski quickly speaks to Mr Nowak in Polish.

'No, we don't know anything. We were at work yesterday, as you know. After you left the farm, we weren't sure what to do, so we went to Wisbech to speak to Mick Mendham, our boss, but he wasn't there. We didn't get back until about eight o'clock and then we saw all the tape and police.'

'What about the other people on the site?' asks Eva.

'There was nobody here: everyone would be at work. If you want to speak to them, you have to come in the evening.'

'Thank you. Does everybody here work for Mick Mendham?'

'Yes,' Mr Kowalski replies, 'everybody except Lena and Alecja. Mick won't have anything to do with them anymore.'

'Why is that?'

'We don't know, it's not our business.'

Steve decides not to pursue the subject. Instead he asks:

'And what about yourselves, what are you going to do?'

'We will be alright,' Mr Kowalski answers. 'There is plenty of work but we want Mick to talk to Mr Jackson's son to see if he needs us to keep the farm going while they sort out what to do next.'

'Thank you. You've been very helpful.' Steve gives them his card. 'If there is anything else you can remember, please call us.'

Mr Kowalski quickly speaks to Mr Nowak and says,

'We can't think of anything.'

After this Steve and Eva leave and make their way to the car.

Just before he starts the engine, Steve receives the message from DCS Sutton so they turn left at the junction and drive back in the direction of Downham Market.

'Well,' says Steve, 'they were friendly enough but we didn't learn anything new.'

'I wouldn't say that,' replies Eva. 'They obviously didn't realise I could understand everything they said to each other. When Mr Kowalski said he and Mr Nowak liked Alecja he was lying because when they were talking in Polish Mr Nowak actually referred to her as Mr Jackson's whore.'

'Phew,' Steve exclaims. 'It could mean Alecja is in fact Mr Jackson's love interest. So there is definitely a connection. Excellent work Eva, I owe you a drink. Did they say anything else?'

'Nothing significant, I think,' replies Eva 'except before we left, Mr Kowalski said to Nowak:

"I told you the girl was trouble; I told you it all began before the tractor got stolen and she started to visit Mr Jackson."

9

Alecja sits up. She feels her wrist. A neat bandage has dressed the cut from the broken glass. She stares at it. Who helped her? Who put the bandage on? She feels fuzzy and has a terrible headache. She looks around the room. There is something odd about the walls but she can't work out what. A stream of sunlight illuminates the room through a window, too high up for her to reach. She carefully gets up from the settee and makes it to the door. She tries to open it but it is locked. She wants to scream but no sound comes out of her mouth. She starts crying. What is happening?

When she's made it back onto the settee, she hears a key turning. The door slowly opens. In comes a man wearing a balaclava. He's carrying a bag which he empties on the little table next to the settee. There's a flask of coffee and a couple of sandwiches. She suddenly realises how hungry she is.

'Thank you.' she whispers.

'Eat.' he tells her. She bites into the bread but finds it difficult to swallow. She drinks some of the coffee.

Her throat is dry and painful. But I must eat, she tells herself, I must be strong.

'Why are you keeping me locked up?' she whispers when she has finished.

'Don't worry: you won't be here for long. You're moving tonight.' He walks over to her. She realises she doesn't have the strength to fight him so offers no resistance when he says:

'Let's have a look at your wrist.'

He takes her hand but instead of looking at the wound he produces a syringe. Before she truly realises what's happening, he plants the needle in her arm. She wants to scream 'NO,' but after only a few minutes, a warm flow of contentment washes over her and soon after, she closes her eyes and falls back on the settee.

10

When they arrive back at the station, Eva agrees to quickly nip to Greggs to get a ham and cheese toastie for Steve and a bacon wrap for herself. Steve makes his way to DCS Sutton's office, already anticipating the taste of good coffee. He realises he has gone without a drink for at least five hours.

The Detective Chief Superintendent is waiting for him and Steve immediately picks up on a change in her demeanour. She appears excited. Wait until you hear what I've got to say, he thinks to himself. He explains Eva has gone to get them something to eat. Sarah Sutton picks up the phone and tells Maddy:

'As soon as PC Lappinska is back, can you ask her to come to join us? She can bring the food with her. They can eat it in my office!'

This is a first, Steve realises. In all the time he has worked with Sarah she has always insisted the canteen is for eating and the office is for working. Also, she is a strict vegan and objects to the smell of meat. But he doesn't say anything except a short,

'Thank you.'

Sarah turns to Steve.

'Glad you are back so early. Before Eva joins us, I want to fill you in on what my thoughts are.'
She proceeds to tell Steve of her unease and her sense that there is of lack of urgency. She explains she wants to go public in the hope someone might come forward with more information but she is prepared to wait until after receiving feedback from everyone else. She also tells him she has asked for further backup.

'What do you think?'

'I totally agree,' Steve replies, 'especially after what we've found out today.' He continues by telling what Eva overheard from the two farmworkers.

'So you were right,' Sarah exclaims, 'there is a connection. This puts a whole new perspective on the case and definitely means we have to step up our efforts considerably. Like you, I am almost certain we are dealing with the same people, the same criminals. And if they were cold-blooded enough to kill Jimmy Jackson, I am seriously worried about the welfare of Miss Tobinska. Well done Steve, you showed good instincts.'
This is what he likes about her, Steve thinks, she might challenge you but she is also generous with her praise when it's been warranted.

'It is Eva who deserves the praise,' he replies.

At the same moment, the woman he's just mentioned joins them and they continue with a more general discussion about the morning's events.

About halfway through, Sergeant Newman calls and asks if they can borrow Eva as PC Sheldon has found a thread in Polish on Alecja Tobinska's Facebook page he thinks might be significant.

By three o'clock everybody is back at the station and there is an air of excitement in the room. Although nobody is exactly sure what's going on, the arrival of the three colleagues from Cambridgeshire, as well as the three extra officers from Norfolk, indicates something is definitely afoot.

DCS Sutton welcomes the regular team to the meeting room and explains the most important development of the day: that they now have a strong indication there is a link between Alecja Tobinska and Jimmy Jackson. But she warns:

'Until we have the pathologist's report, we cannot be certain his death is suspicious. However,' she continues, 'from now on, we proceed as if it is. It means we believe Alecja Tobinska is in grave danger and all our efforts must be on finding her as soon as possible. DCI Culverhouse, will you continue please?'

Steve stands up and briefly recounts their visit to

the caravan site and what they have learnt.

'It is important we return later and speak to the other people who live there.' He turns to DI Woods:

'Anything from Wisbech?'

'Nothing substantial,' the Detective Inspector replies. 'We found out there's plenty of work: the agencies can't get enough staff. Also, after getting the message from Sergeant Newman, we concentrated on trying to locate Mick Mendham. It was actually easier than we thought. Where some gangmasters keep themselves to themselves, Mick appears quite open and proud of his business interests. He owns a farm at Leverington and has a big sign outside the drive to his property advertising himself as Mick Mendham, Church Farm Enterprises. However, he was not at home when we called at the farm office. His secretary said he was away for a few days but would be back on Thursday. She had no idea where he was and said she could not contact him.'

Two days until Thursday, Steve thinks, we haven't got that much time. He turns to Sergeant Newman:

'Dave, have you got anything to add?'

'Mr Mendham has his fingers in a lot of pies,' he replies. 'On his website, he lists his enterprises as Mick Mendham, Employment Solutions, Mick Mendham, Agricultural Contractor and Mick

Mendham, New and Used Farm Machinery.'

Steve's ears prick up when he hears the last bit and he immediately thinks of the missing tractor.

'Anything else?'

'PC Sheldon found something that might be of interest,' he replies and nods to his colleague to continue.

'There is a thread on Facebook between Alecja and some friends back in Poland, which Eva kindly translated. In it, she hints her fortunes may have changed for the better. She talks about meeting someone and suggests her money worries might soon be over. At one point, she promises she will tell more on their WhatsApp group. But as those conversations are encrypted, we have no access to them. Oh, and her cousin was not party to this thread. In fact, she is not listed as one of Alecja's Facebook friends.'

'You're right,' DI Starling chips in, 'Lena told me she does not have Facebook, only Instagram, and communicates with her family through WhatsApp and text messages only.'

'Thank you, PC Sheldon.'

Steve turns to DI Starling:

'What else have you found out?'

'Lena is extremely concerned. I think as the older of the two, she feels somehow a bit responsible for her cousin. But also, they do not appear to be as close as you might think. Yes, they go out together occasionally but not all the time. I think, and this is only my impression, Lena feels Alecja sometimes courts trouble a bit too much.'

Interesting, thinks Steve. It ties in with other things he has heard today.

'But in terms of factual information, we did not get a lot further.'

DI Starling continues to give an account of their conversation in King's Lynn, followed by a brief outline of the follow-up interview at the police station.

'I asked her why she didn't ring 999 or seek help from the other people on the site. Well, apparently she did try to get help but everybody was out. As for not ringing, she explained she was scared and wanted to get away from the place as soon as possible.

'DI Baker, do you have anything to add?'

'I agree with DI Starling,' he replies. 'She did appear a little disappointed in her cousin but I can't put my finger on why. It wasn't anything she said so much, more the way she went about saying things. And I also think she is petrified of this guy Curly. We have to find out in what way he and Mick Mendham are connected.'

'Good point,' Steve cuts in and turning to DI Wood and PC Redding, he asks:

'Did you find anything out about this guy Curly?'

Slightly embarrassed, PC Redding turns to DI Woods.

'I'm sorry, I forgot to mention, in one of the employment agencies, the member of staff I talked to said someone named Curly occasionally visited them when he needed extra staff. She also said she didn't know much about him but he wasn't British and originally came from the Netherlands.'

'Useful to know,' Steve replies. 'It should help us in locating him. Any more questions?'

'When are we getting the pathologist's report?' John Baker asks.

'Ah,' says DCS Sutton, 'we've been promised it later on today or tomorrow morning at the latest.'

After establishing no-one has further questions, DCS Sutton suggests:

'Take a break everyone, can we all be back here at four o'clock including our colleagues from Norfolk and Cambridge? Maddy and Steve, can you come to my office please?'

They follow her up to her office. When they are about to sit down, the phone rings. DCS Sutton indicates for them to leave again. After five minutes, she opens the door and invites Steve back in. 'That was the pathologist,' she says by way of explanation.

'She rang to share her preliminary findings. Jimmy Jackson died of natural causes. Apparently, he had a massive heart attack leading to almost instant death.'

'But I don't understand!' Steve replies, bewildered. 'If he had a heart attack, how could he have shot himself?'

'He couldn't,' answers DCS Sutton. 'Some sick bastard took his dead body, propped it up against the tractor and blasted his face off.'

11

Twenty minutes later, Steve and DCS Sutton are again joined by the other three detectives. Sarah explains she has tasked Maddie to design a "missing person" poster to be used in the search for Alecja. She fills them in on the latest developments and glances around the room.

'We need a plan of action and we need it quick.' She opens her laptop and continues, 'I'll make notes myself. Steve, you start.'

'The priority has to be finding Ms Tobinska,' says Steve, 'and for that purpose, we now need to go public. As DCS Sutton says, Maddy is printing the posters as we speak. I suggest we involve radio, TV, social media and the newspapers as soon as possible. All the door-to-door stuff can be done by the extra officers we have available. They'll need a thorough briefing, though.'

'That can be done as part of our four o'clock meeting,' interjects DCS Sutton.

'Next, we need to find out the places Alecja used to visit. DI Starling, can you contact Lena and tell her what's going on and get some more information on where they used to hang out?'

'No problem,' says DI Starling, 'Lena is still here. I didn't have time to take her back to Lynn, so I asked her to wait downstairs.'

'Great,' Steve replies. 'That should save some time. In the meantime, I think the rest of us should concentrate on following up on the work we did today. DI Woods, I want you to go back to Wisbech and find the woman who knew Curly and see if you can get some more information. Also, put some pressure on Mr Mendham's secretary and get at least a mobile contact number out of her. You better leave straight away; otherwise, they might have gone home by the time you get there. If anything else crops up, we'll be in touch.' DI Woods nods, gets up and leaves the room.

'DI Baker, you stay here and coordinate a rota for staffing the phones and Facebook messages in case we get a response from the public. Talk to Maddy; she will help and set it up. Don't forget to get in touch with the control room at Police Headquarters in Wymondham and inform them of what we are doing. Also, can you and maybe DI Starling deploy our extra staff to start the house-to-house? I myself

70

will go to Nordelph and talk to Jimmy's family again. They must be wondering what is happening and it's best to get to them before the rumours start flying. I presume, DCS Sutton that you are going to take charge of the media yourself?'

'I will,' she replies. 'I think we should keep it short and to the point, without alarming people too much and alerting the criminals behind this that we are on to them. I agree with Steve that all of us here should be on our way as soon as possible after our four o'clock meeting so we get out there before this stuff hits the news. Make sure you keep your mobiles charged and switched on and I will see you all back here in about half an hour.'

After they've left, DCS Sutton pours herself a coffee and takes stock. She feels much better because, although the news has been terrible and they are almost certainly dealing with a major crime, at least things have started moving and there are several leads to follow up. She next picks up the phone and dials the number of Alan Phelan at *The Fenland Gazette*.

Well before four o'clock everyone is assembled in the conference room. DCS Sutton thanks them all for coming. She introduces PCs Sheldon, Lappinska and Redding to the recently arrived officers from the other forces and asks them to address any questions they may have to these three officers first. She continues by filling in the background to the case and why she has asked them all to join.

Next, she shares the preliminary findings of the pathologist before saying:

'Until we get the full report, we cannot say for certain what has happened or why. However, it is clear we are dealing with some particularly nasty individuals here. Because of that, we must be careful not to give too much away in our dealings with the public. As far as you are concerned, you are engaging in a missing person search, not a criminal investigation. But of course, keep your eyes and ears open and report anything, however trivial, back to the station. Good luck everyone.'

Finally she introduces DI Baker, who will organise the assembled officers and allocate them to specific geographical areas and places, based on the information DI Starling has supplied him with after talking to Lena.

The press conference is scheduled for five o'clock. This will allow both local TV news channels to carry the item and give the newspapers the opportunity to include it in the daily updates on their websites and Twitter feeds.

At exactly five o'clock, DCS Sutton makes her way to the meeting room, which has been readied to be used for the press conference. She is wearing the black and grey business suit she keeps at the station for exactly this sort of eventuality and has put on a clean, freshly ironed white shirt. She has touched up the little make-up she wears and brushed her hair. She is ready.

When she enters the room and walks to the desk at the front, she casts her eye over the assembled journalists. It always impresses her how quickly they are able to attend a hastily convened press conference such as this. She nods to Alan Phelan, who sits next to his colleagues from the *Lynn News,* the *Wisbech Standard* and the *Eastern Daily Press.* The BBC have sent their *Look East* correspondent from King's Lynn, who will cover the news broadcast at six-thirty as well as filing a report for the *Drive Time Show* on Radio Norfolk. *Anglia Today* is represented by one of their reporters from Cambridge, who must have cut it fine to be here in time unless he was in the area already.

She welcomes everybody and thanks them for coming. She explains she will read from a pre-prepared statement and everyone present will receive a copy of this, after which there will be time to ask questions. She pauses before she picks up the paper in front of her.

'The Fenland Police Force is asking for your cooperation in finding a missing person. It is believed thirty-two year old Alecja Tobinska left her home in the Outwell area sometime yesterday. She has not been seen since. We have reason to believe she is injured and might need medical help. We are asking anyone who may have seen her, or can inform us of her whereabouts, to get in touch with us as soon as possible.'

She passes the paper around the room and continues:

'Our contact details are included in the press release. Thank you, any questions anyone?'
Several of the journalists raise their hands. Sarah points at Alan Phelan.

'Isn't it unusual to make a public appeal so quickly after an adult disappears? Does this suggest there is more to,' he checks his notes, 'Miss Tobinska's disappearance than a simple missing person case?'

'Like I said, the reason for our concern is that she might be injured and needs medical attention,' DCS Sutton replies, 'but I cannot give you details of the nature of these injuries as we simply don't know at this moment in time.'

'What makes you believe she is injured?' another journalist asks.

'I'm afraid I can't disclose that at present.'

'Where does she live? You say the Outwell area but that could mean anywhere between here and Wisbech.'

'You are right,' DCS Sutton replies, 'but we currently have teams of officers conducting door-to-door enquiries. Until they have finished, we won't be disclosing the exact location of Miss Tobinska's home.' She smiles. 'After all, if we did, you'd all be in your cars by now making your way there.' This produces a ripple of laughter.

'If that is all, I'd like to thank you for coming. Before you go, please leave your details with Mrs Bowen at the information desk and we will make sure you are being kept informed if and when we have further news. Thank you.'

She leaves the room but before going up to her office has a quick word with Mrs Bowen to see if she is alright.

'Of course I am,' says Maddy, 'and don't worry, I'll stay as long as necessary. I've already rung my husband to tell him he better get some supper for himself. And guess what? He's going to get an Indian take-away and drop one off for me too. I've gone for a vegetable biryani, my favourite.'

Sarah smiles. It must be nice to have a thoughtful

partner like Mrs Bowen's husband. She has not been so lucky but, as she reminds herself, you can't have everything. At the moment, she definitely wouldn't have the time to fit a partner into her busy life.

Before she goes upstairs to phone and update the Deputy Chief Constable, Sarah pops into the kitchen and puts a ready-made vegan lasagne in the microwave. '*This will have to do for me,*' she tells herself without a hint of self-pity.

12

DI Woods is not having much luck. He's checked the opening hours of the recruitment agency where PC Redding spoke to the member of staff about the mysterious Curly and found it didn't close until seven-thirty. 'Result!' he said to himself, 'It gives me plenty of time to drive to Leverington first and visit Mick Mendham's office.'

But when he gets there, he finds the gates closed and no way of getting in. He gets out his mobile phone and rings the number he'd written down during his previous visit. No luck. He decides against leaving a message and drives back to Wisbech. Now he finds himself in a line of people, all waiting to be seen by the two members of staff who are doing their best to deal with everyone as quickly as possible. It sounds like the United Nations in here, he thinks to himself, listening to several languages being spoken at once. For a brief moment he wonders about showing his warrant card to get first in the queue but decides against it. There's nothing to be gained at the moment from letting on that the police are looking for both Mick Mendham and Curly. Instead, he leaves the agency and makes himself comfortable in the café opposite with a cup of tea and a bacon roll. He gets his phone out and rings the agency. After quite a few rings, a man answers.

'Can I speak to your colleague, please?' asks DI Woods.

'Which one?' the man replies. 'There's five of us here.'

'The female downstairs, please.'

'What, you want to speak to one of our female staff and you don't know her name? What are you, her stalker?'

This is all going wrong, DI Woods realises. He kicks himself; why didn't he contemplate there might be more staff elsewhere in the building?

'No,' he says. 'It's nothing like that, I came in earlier and need to ask her a quick question and there is a long queue and I'm in a bit of a hurry.'

'Tell you what,' the man suggests. 'You give me your number and I'll ask her to ring you back when she's free. As you said yourself, she's busy and I don't see why you should jump the queue.' DI Woods realises he's got little choice but to wait, so he gives the man his number and concentrates on enjoying his food.

While Steve is driving towards the Jacksons' he thinks back over the last two days. Was it only yesterday morning that he first crossed the bridge at Nordelph? He navigates the tight corner and drives along the bumpy Silt Road. Before long, Jimmy Jackson's farm comes in sight and soon after, Steve turns into the drive of the substantial barn conversion, home to Jack Jackson and his family. To the right of the drive is an open garage with space for four cars. He can see a black BMW, the black Audi he'd seen yesterday when Marion arrived at the farm and a black Range Rover. He has phoned ahead and as soon as he opens the car door, he is greeted by Jack himself.

'Thank you for coming. Is there any news from the coroner?' And without waiting for an answer, 'When will my dad's body be released so we can plan the funeral?' Before interrupting himself and saying, 'Sorry, come in, Marion is making tea. Let's go through to the lounge.'

Once they are seated, Steve explains he does have some news he wishes to share but before he does, he asks if the children are likely to come into the room.

'Don't worry,' says Marion. 'They are spending the

week with my parents in Peterborough. We thought it was best for them and it gives us a chance to concentrate on what to do next. Jimmy's death means we have to focus on what happens now with the farm and all that.'

Marion has definitely recovered from her shock yesterday and appears much more composed. Just as well, Steve thinks to himself, seeing as what I'm going to have to tell them.

'Indeed,' he says, 'it must all be overwhelming.' He continues: 'The reason I've come to see you is that there are some developments. The pathologist has done her work and has given us a brief outline of her findings. I am afraid it throws up more questions than answers. It now appears Mr Jackson - sorry, your father - died of a heart attack.'

'What does that mean?' Jack cries as the enormity of this statement slowly dawns on him. 'If he died of a heart attack, how could he shoot himself? What, I saw him lying there, I saw the gun!'

Marion takes his hand and squeezes it.

'Are you saying my father-in-law was shot after he died?' she asks. 'Surely that can't be possible, there must be some mistake and they must have got it wrong.'

'I am sorry. I find it pretty unbelievable myself but

until we get the full report, I can't tell you any more. I wanted to tell you myself before it gets out into the public domain.'

'Thank you,' Marion replies quietly.

'It does mean the farm needs to be sealed off for a few more days. Do you have any livestock that need looking after?' Jack shakes his head.

'Okay,' Steve says. 'I will come back as soon as we have the full pathologist's report. I will also introduce you to our family liaison officer, who will act as your direct point of contact in case you have any questions. For now, feel free to contact me directly. You still have my number?'
Marion nods.

And with that, Steve takes his leave, saying:

'Don't get up, I'll let myself out.' He walks back to his car realising how much he hates being the bearer of bad news.

He turns left out of the drive and spontaneously indicates right and ends up back at Jimmy Jackson's farm. Everything is exactly as he left it the day before but he is aware of how isolated the house is on this empty road with the late afternoon sunshine slowly fading away. He rings DCS Sutton, who agrees with him that they should deploy some of the extra officers to keep an eye on the place. She suggests they do the same with the mobile home of the Tobinska cousins.

By five o'clock, DI Baker has instructed and dispatched most of the police constables. He himself has agreed to stay with Sergeant Newman at the station to respond to any calls from the public after the news has been broadcast. DI Starling and one of the police constables are going back to King's Lynn, where they will drop Lena off at her friend's house.

This leaves PC Lappinska, who together with PC Ben Sheldon will visit the caravan site in Nordelph again. Sheldon has volunteered to take the first shift, keeping an eye on the mobile home. But as it might still be a little early for all the workers to return home, DI Baker suggests that they should start with a door-to-door of the houses on Silt Road, in case anyone noticed anything unusual. The two remaining officers are told they are assigned to Jimmy Jackson's farm. One of them lives only a few miles away in the village of Fincham and is to go home and get some sleep while the other one, taking the first shift, is promised he will be relieved at midnight.

DI Baker issues all of them with the relevant phone numbers and names and sends everybody on their way. He gets back to his computer to work out the schedule for the coming days.

In the car park, PC Sheldon and his colleague assigned to do the first shift decide they will need to nip to the supermarket and stock up with provisions, ready for what may be a long night ahead of them. Eva suggests they meet somewhere along the Silt Road; no doubt they will see her car parked at one of the few houses and if not, there's always the phone. Eva checks her watch, five o' clock.

At that moment, DCI Culverhouse enters the car park, returning from his visit to the Jacksons. They greet each other and Steve suggests Eva may wish to consider becoming the family liaison officer for Jack Jackson and his wife. It is a role she has carried out before and she has been told she is quite good at.

'No problem,' she replies.

'In that case, we will visit them together tomorrow, as soon as we receive the pathologist's report.'

Half an hour later, Eva is driving along the Silt Road. She decides to go as far as the first junction and make her way back, visiting the few farms and houses dotted along the road between there and Nordelph. She calculates there are maybe twenty properties at the most, so it shouldn't take too long.

Although she hasn't yet visited Jimmy Jackson's farm, Steve told her where it is. Just before she gets there, she notices a car leaving the farm and turning right, coming towards her. Because the setting sun is in her eyes, she has trouble seeing the driver's face. She makes a mental note to tell Steve on her return to the station.

About forty minutes later she is joined by PC Sheldon and his colleague.

'Absolutely nothing,' she tells the others, 'no one has seen or heard anything.'

'I've got it on good authority it was suicide,' one of the farmers had told her. 'Why are you wasting your time knocking on doors when you should be solving crimes instead?' She had sighed, she's heard it all before but it still makes her angry. *If only you knew,* she thinks.

Eva suggests to Ben they first drive to Jimmy Jackson's farm to show their colleague where it is. She is also keen to have a quick look herself. They walk around the farm buildings and make for the house. Eva is aware she doesn't know precisely what she is looking for but everything appears to be in order. They say goodbye to their colleague who has made himself comfortable in his car, parked out of sight, next to the grain store.

When they arrive at the mobile home park, they find lights on in most of the caravans. Eva makes for the one they visited earlier on in the day. There is no sign of anyone being in and, as no one replies to her knock on the door, they decide to start at one end and visit the others one by one.

DI Starling and PC Redding are eating fish and chips

in PC Redding's car. They are parked in Norfolk Street, by day home to a mixture of small independent shops, a few nationals such as Waterstones and WH Smith and an array of charity shops. By night the street completely changes character and comes to life with groups of young people queuing outside a number of nightclubs or simply hanging around a series of kebab and pizza places. It is here that PC Redding is often deployed when working out of King's Lynn Police Station. At this time of a Tuesday evening, it is fairly quiet as the two most popular clubs don't open until nine o'clock. Also, people haven't started drinking yet. It will be totally different in about four to five hours' time but both police officers hope they will have gotten home long before then.

After finishing their food, DI Starling suggests each take one side of the street and leave posters in the food outlets and pubs while trying to find out whether or not the bar staff recognise Alecja from the posters. Lena has told her the cousins would normally visit *Tramways*, one of the two clubs with later opening hours.

'Why that particular one?' DI Starling had asked.

'Because they are more tolerant of foreigners in there,' Lena said before adding, 'but Alecja enjoyed clubbing much more than I do, so she often went out on her own. Maybe she didn't go to the same place every time.'

So each armed with a stack of posters, PC Redding and DI Starling set off from the town end of the street to make their way towards the junction with Railway Road, after which the road becomes much quieter.

After Eva has left, Steve heads inside and makes for the kitchen where he retrieves a cheese sandwich from the fridge. He feels hungry and it's quite likely he will have to forego supper tonight. He joins DCS Sutton and DI Baker in the conference room, where they are waiting for the local news to start. Steve consults his watch, another twenty minutes. He fills the other detectives in on his visit to the Jacksons, finishing with his suggestion that PC Lappinska should act as family liaison officer.

'Good call,' DCS Sutton replies minutes before *Anglia Today* appears on the screen. When both local news programmes are finished Steve and DCS Sutton find themselves sharing a coffee and taking stock. So far, the press release has yielded a paltry response of six callers, most of them fellow workers from Alecja's time at the canning factory, saying they know who she is but haven't seen her for a while. One person is convinced they saw her in

Norwich on Monday morning, getting off the train from London at seven-thirty. This sighting is quickly dismissed as this was the time she was talking to her cousin before she disappeared. Finally, another caller says he doesn't know her but asked if the police could give her his number when she is found as he would like to take her out on a date. DI Baker, who took the call, firmly informed the caller that wasting police time was a criminal offence, which was greeted by laughter on the other end of the line.

DI Woods has rung in, explaining his predicament. He did not receive a phone call from the woman in the recruitment agency, so he went back ten minutes before closing time at seven-thirty. There were only two people in front of him but by the time he got to the desk, he was told that the woman he wished to speak to had gone home at six-thirty.

'Blast!' he said to himself. He should have kept a more careful eye on the place.

'What's done is done,' Steve told him over the phone. 'You might as well go home; you're halfway to Long Sutton already. Check what time they open and pop in on your way to work tomorrow morning.'

The two officers assigned to visit the pubs and clubs in Wisbech have had more success. Most of the cafés and takeaway shops they visited were more than happy to help and several of them immediately put the "missing" poster in their windows. When they visited *Barka,* a relatively small club on a converted barge, moored on the river Nene, the owner himself took an interest.

'I recognise her. She used to be a regular here but I have not seen her for a couple of weeks. Nice girl, good-looking too,' he smiled.

'Did she come on her own or with friends?'

'I only ever saw her on her own. We are a friendly club: women can come on their own and feel safe. We have mainly Eastern European customers and we look after each other.'

'How would she spend an evening?' one of the officers asked.

'What I remember is she used to always quickly have someone to chat to and dance with.
Like I said, she is a good-looking girl.'

'Did you ever see her leave with anyone?' the officers asked.

'Not that I can remember but you better ask Kacper, our regular doorman. But he's not here right now. He only works on weekends: we don't need a bouncer during the week.'

Not much, DCS Sutton concludes, but it is not too dissimilar to the report she has received from DI

Starling in King's Lynn. Apparently, Alecja frequented the *Tramways* club on Norfolk Street regularly, both on her own or with her cousin. However, over the last few months, the visits had become less frequent and if she did come, it was only when she was with her cousin.

DI Starling had rung Lena and asked her about this.

'I didn't know she had stopped going on her own,' she said, 'maybe she went to another club like I said before. She definitely went out as often as she used to.'

Again DI Starling got the feeling the cousins were not as close as you might have expected in the case of two young women living together in a foreign country. She remembered living with her sister in London for a year during her police training. They would always tell each other what they had been up to the night before.

Eva's report had been short and to the point. The house-to-house inquiries had not yielded any information and although the people in the mobile homes had been friendly, no one had seen or heard anything. They all knew Curly by sight, as at one point he regularly visited the site in his shiny black Range Rover, but that was all. No one had a bad word to say about Mick Mendham. He was a fair boss, they said, who would pay his regular employees even when they couldn't work due to bad weather, unlike some of the other gangmasters. Eva finished by telling DCI Culverhouse about the four-by-four coming out of Jimmy Jackson's drive when she was passing. She added she thought nothing at the farm looked like it was disturbed.

'We'll have a look tomorrow on our way to the Jacksons,' Steve replied. 'It does make me feel better that we are now guarding the place.'

And that was it, DCS Sutton thought, two days and no real progress. She sent everybody home except DI Baker, who offered to man the phones until nine o'clock.

Maybe something will come in overnight, she hoped. Steve and she had agreed the first priority tomorrow must be to talk to Mick Mendham and Curly. Also, the pathologist's report might shine some more light on Jimmy Jackson's death. She poured herself another coffee and waited until nine o'clock when DI Baker knocked on her door to say goodbye. They walked together to the car park and made their way home.

13

When Alecja opens her eyes, the room is dark. Someone is shining a torch in her face.

'Ah, you're awake,' she hears the now familiar voice behind the balaclava say to her. 'Can you try to get up?' She feels two strong arms help her stand up straight. 'Don't worry, I'm holding you,' she hears the man say.

'Where are we going?' she asks.

'Away from here,' comes the answer.

'Good,' Alecja whispers.

The man gently puts a blindfold over her eyes and they make their way outside onto a kind of balcony.

'Careful on the steps,' the man warns. The fresh air almost overwhelms her and she nearly slips but makes it safely to the bottom of the stairs. The man guides her to a car. She doesn't have the strength to protest. She gets in and half curls over on the back seat. The man starts the engine and they drive for maybe half an hour before she feels the car turning on to a bumpy track. After only a short while, they come to a stop. The man helps her out of the car and tells her she can take the blindfold off. In the dark, she sees the outline of a small building. He takes her arm and they walk to the door. He undoes the lock and they step inside. Once there, he lights an old-fashioned oil lamp. She remembers seeing one of these at her grandparents' house back in Poland. She starts crying.

'Don't cry,' the man says, 'don't worry, I'm looking after you. I need you to get strong and healthy again.' He gives her a banana and puts the rest of the bunch on a small table next to a bottle of water. She eats the banana and takes a swig of water. She looks around and notices that there is a rudimentary toilet in the corner.

While she is eating, the man sets up a metal camp bed and produces a pillow and a couple of sleeping bags from a black bin liner.

'This should keep you warm.'

He helps her onto the bed and once again produces a small syringe. She doesn't fight it but almost embraces the feeling of warmth when the drug enters her veins.

WEDNESDAY

14

The next morning, Steve arrives at the station early. He has a slight hangover, probably from drinking one too many Irish whiskeys the night before and spending an uncomfortable couple of hours on the sofa, where he had dozed off before summoning up the energy to get himself upstairs and into his own bed.

He'd arrived at his house just before nine o'clock after picking up a Thai curry on the way home from the police station. As soon as he got in, his phone rang. It was Julia who wanted reassurance Steve was still free the coming weekend so they could go to the coast for a few days.

'I'm sorry,' Steve had said, 'we've got a big case on. Unless we have a result before Friday, I can't guarantee it.'

'I sometimes think you don't want us to come up anymore,' Julia had replied.

Was it his imagination or did she sound just a little relieved the weekend might not go ahead?

'How are the boys?' he had asked.

'If you came down a bit more often,' Julia had said, 'you could see for yourself. And they both have phones, you know!' Before long, the conversation had turned into a row finishing with Julia telling him she'd had enough and if he wanted to see them, he would have to start taking the initiative. She was no longer prepared to have her plans scuppered week after week. Her final words were, 'It's not all about you. I also have a life, you know!' And then she'd put the phone down.

The unopened curry had gone cold, so Steve put it in the microwave. He ate without tasting it much, before settling into his armchair and opening a new bottle of Bushmills. Julia was right, of course: too many weekends had been cancelled because of his work. But that was the nature of the job. She had known this when she married him. As for the boys, he tried to justify his lack of communication with them to himself but he knew deep inside he found it more and more difficult to relate. Every time he saw them, they had grown and changed further. When he talked to them on the phone, they quickly ran out of things to say. They would talk about friends he didn't know and teachers he'd never met. They had no hobbies in common. Both boys were into computer games in a big way, something Steve didn't understand and had no interest in. His own hobbies were more sport orientated, football from the comfort of his armchair and road cycling as exercise were his favourites. He felt guilty, though, and promised himself he would make more of an effort in the future.

He had tried to ring Julia back but she hadn't picked up. So instead, he had sent her a text message, suggesting they could talk the following evening. By the time he'd done that it was past eleven o'clock, so he had poured himself another whiskey while searching for John Martin's *Solid Air* on his Spotify playlist.

In spite of the bad night and unsettling conversation the previous evening, Steve is looking forward to the distraction of going back to work. He arrives at the car park at the same time as DCS Sutton. He switches his computer on and checks the link with Wymondham Police Headquarters. Nothing! No new sightings or other information. Next, he jots down some of the things that have been playing on his mind including his belief that the theft of the tractor might somehow be a factor in all this. But he has no idea how and why.

'Can you join me please?' he hears DCS Sutton calling out. He picks up his notes and makes his way up to her office.

'The pathologist's report has arrived,' she says. 'They must have been working late last night. It was sent at twelve-thirty.'

'And?' Steve inquires.

'I think it's best if you read it for yourself,' she replies and turns her laptop around so Steve can see the screen.

He quickly scans the first couple of pages until he gets to the description of the injuries and cause of death. 'Bloody hell!' he remarks.

'I see you've found it,' Sarah comments. 'Coffee? I think we need to have a bit of a think about our next steps and priorities.'

Steve agrees. The report is roughly in line with the preliminary findings from the day before but with one big exception. It now appears Jimmy Jackson was not only shot but also subjected to a botched attempt to strangle him. Marks on his neck and fibres found there suggest this might have been done with bailing twine. Similar fibres and scratches were found on both his wrists, which suggests he would have had his hands tied. In the email accompanying the report, the pathologist suggests it is most likely Jimmy had his heart attack while they were trying to strangle him. But as this is speculation, she has not included her opinion in the official report.

'Let's go to the incident room,' Sarah suggests after they've finished their coffee. She takes off the two sheets on the flipchart where Steve had previously written MURDER? SUICIDE?

'We now know what it is,' she says. 'Although Mr Jackson's death may factually not be murder, we will treat it as such for all intents and purposes. Steve, I'm aware you thought this from the beginning but I too am now convinced Ms Tobinska's disappearance is connected to Jimmy Jackson's murder. And to me, her disappearance is looking more and more like the actions of someone who is deliberately hiding somewhere. For all we know she might be back in Poland already.'

Steve nods; he has had the same thoughts himself. Was Alecja involved in Jimmy's murder? Is that why she went missing? Or did she know too much and was therefore forced to disappear? He shares these thoughts with DCS Sutton, who agrees but says:

'Either way, finding Alecja appears to be key to finding out who is behind all this. But if she was involved in the murder, she could not have done it on her own. From what you have told me, Jimmy Jackson was a big man and she would not have had the strength.'

'Let's start at the beginning.' DCS Sutton says when DI Starling and DI Baker have joined them.

'John, you make notes,' she continues, as she hands DI Baker the marker pens they use on the flipcharts.

'Facts please,' she says invitingly to the others: they've worked this kind of brainstorming session in the past and it isn't long before DI Baker struggles to keep up.

"Jimmy Jackson is dead, strangled and shot."

"Alecja Tobinska disappears the same day."

"Alecja and Jimmy were quite possibly in a romantic relationship."

"Jimmy Jackson had some bad luck with his tractor being stolen and problems with the potato harvest."

"Alecja used to work for Jimmy Jackson."

"Alecja has a bit of a reputation of being difficult."

"Alecja was in debt to Mick Mendham."

"Mick Mendham no longer deals with Alecja."

"Alecja is also in debt to Curly."

"We don't know who Curly is."

"Alecja got the sack from Jimmy's farm between the bad potato harvest and the theft of the tractor."

"Could the motive be revenge, was she involved in the theft of the tractor?"

"Alecja, in spite of being sacked by him, starts a possible affair with Jimmy, a man twice her age."

'That will do,' says DCS Sutton, calling the brainstorming session to a halt. 'If you think of any more during the day, just add them.'
They sit in silence for a while, looking at the sheets of paper in front of them before DCS Sutton says:
'Grab yourselves a drink and we'll continue in a few minutes.'

When the four of them return to the room, Sutton invites each of them to interpret the factual information they have put together. Steve is aware she will already have digested all the info herself and probably have a strategy at the ready, but he appreciates the fact she is open to other people's suggestions.

DS Starling starts by saying that in her opinion, the main focus should remain on finding Alecja, but in order to do so, they must urgently speak to both Mick Mendham and Curly.

DS Baker points out Alecja is the common thread through everything that has happened over the last few months.

When Steve is invited to speak, he suggests they should start at the beginning.

'And where is that?' DCS Sutton asks.

'I think it has something to do with what happened at the time the tractor was stolen. If we could find out more about that, I'm sure we would get a lot further by establishing a motive for the other events. But I agree with the others, Ms Tobinska's welfare is the most important thing at the moment and we must find her as soon as possible.'

When Steve has finished speaking, they all turn to DCS Sutton, who thanks them.

'I agree with all of you. There is no doubt in my mind that once we find Mick Mendham and Curly, we will be a lot closer to finding Alecja. And even if she disappeared of her own accord, these two gentlemen will no doubt be of use in solving some of the other questions we are dealing with. For what it's worth, I don't think Mr Jackson's death was premeditated murder. I believe it is most likely the result of something else going disastrously wrong. Thank you everybody. It's eight-thirty: let's rally the troops.'

15

Steve and Eva are driving along the now familiar route to Jack and Marian Jackson's house.

'Wow,' says Eva when they arrive, 'what a lovely place. This must have cost a fair bit.'
Steve agrees: it is a stylish barn conversion, no doubt architect-designed, and it doesn't look as they have cut any corners on quality.

Jack and Marian are waiting for them in the large farmhouse kitchen. Steve introduces Eva and fills them in on the extra detail from the pathologist's report.

'That is so awful, poor Jimmy,' Marian says and starts crying. Jack shows little emotion but stares stony-faced into the distance.

'Bastards,' he says quietly. 'Wait until I get my hands on them.'

'You realise there will be a fair bit of publicity. I would prefer it if you didn't speak to any journalists.

It might be worth shutting your gate to stop them coming too close to the house.'

Jack nods as Steve continues:

'I'm aware you have a lot to cope with at the moment but I need to ask you if you recognise this woman?' He produces one of the "Missing" posters with the picture of Alecja on it.

'I do,' Jack replies. 'She worked for my dad for a few months. Do you think she is involved in all this?'

'We don't know,' Steve replies, 'but she disappeared the same day your father was found. We need to talk to her urgently.'

Nobody speaks for a while until Steve says:

'I suggest we leave you to yourselves now and let it all sink in. PC Lappinska will come back later and answer any further questions you may have.'

'When will we be able to get in the house?' Marian asks. She has stopped crying and is looking more composed.

'I need to get to some of his papers to deal with the bank.'

'We are carrying out another search today. Once that is done, PC Lappinska can accompany you to collect your paperwork.'

And with that, he and Eva say goodbye, leaving Jack and Marion with their thoughts. They get back in Steve's car. When they get to the road, they see the

SOCO van turning into Jimmy Jackson's farm drive.

Before long, they arrive at the NFU office, where Charlie Goodyear is waiting for them.

'Nice to see you again, Inspector, and good morning to you, Miss,' he says. 'I just heard the news on the radio, it's a sad world we live in. I must say, poor Jimmy, he wouldn't harm anyone and poor Jack and Marion, they must be devastated.'

'Ah, you know Mr Jackson's son and daughter-in-law?'

'Oh yes,' Charlie replies. 'Jack often helps me out with all this Brexit paperwork.'

'Sorry?' says Steve, 'I don't understand.'

'Simple,' he replies. 'Jack is an expert on animal passports and such like. He used to have a veterinary practice in March but he sold that to concentrate on setting up his licensing business, getting the right paperwork in place for the transport of live animals between the UK and Europe. Very profitable it is as well, I would think. Well, that whole caboodle, especially the need for pet passports, is getting more and more complicated, especially as Brexit means more charges and extra paperwork. But Jack knows his business. Mind you, he still works as a vet for a day a week at his old practice - to keep his hand in, I suppose. But I'm sure you're not here to talk about Jack?'

'No,' Steve replies. 'I wanted to check if you remembered anything else from when you saw Jimmy in the pub with his lady friend.' Eva is surprised: she had not expected Steve to use such old-fashioned language to describe a modern young woman.

'Not a thing,' Charlie replies. 'I'm sure I told you everything last time we met.'

'In that case,' Steve suggests, 'can you tell us what you know about tractor theft?'

'Where do I start?' Charlie says. 'It's a real nuisance and it's costing the NFU literally millions in insurance pay-outs.'

'Who's behind it all?' Steve asks.

'Nobody knows exactly. The NFU has done some research nationwide and it appears the Turkish and Polish Mafia are the main culprits as far as farm machinery is concerned. These groups are based in rural areas themselves, so they have a ready market for agricultural machinery.

But in the last few years, there's also been a considerable increase in stealing GPS systems from tractors, which we think might be done by more locally based criminals and sold within the country. This has got so bad that we are now advising all farmers to use a PIN code for access. I was told by a colleague from Devon at our conference in London last year that the police there caught a gang red-handed. They were all from the Birmingham area and there wasn't an obvious link to Eastern Europe or Turkey. These criminals cause a lot of damage by breaking windscreens and using crowbars to get in.'

'So how do they get the tractors out of the country?'

'Most of the time, they use false paperwork, put them on a low loader and take the ferry from Harwich to the Hoek van Holland or Hull to Rotterdam. Although we have no proof, we also think that occasionally they simply load the machinery onto one of the coasters bringing timber from Scandinavia into King's Lynn.'

'Do any of the stolen tractors stay in the UK?' Eva asks.

'I'm sure some do,' Charlie replies, 'but I've not heard of any being found around here. If you ask me, Jimmy Jackson's tractor is ploughing some field in Poland as we speak.'

When they get back in the car, Eva asks:

'Can we stop at the petrol station? I could do with a sandwich.'

Steve checks his watch. Twelve-thirty.

'Tell you what. Let's nip to the *Carpenters' Arms* and get something there. I'd like to have a word with the landlady anyway.'

In the pub car park he rings DCS Sutton and fills her

in on what he has learnt so far. He explains his plans for the rest of the afternoon, to which she replies:

'Okay, but can you make sure you're back by 5pm. I'm bringing Mr Kowalski and Mr Nowak in for questioning and want to discuss our approach with you.'

'How so,' Steve asks, 'has anything come up that implicates them?'

'No,' she replies, 'the problem is that nothing has come up, so I'm clutching at straws. But these two found Mr Jackson and lived next door to Ms Tobinska. They might have seen or heard a little more than they have told us so far. By the way, can you ask Eva to be available to translate if necessary, please?'

After lunch, Steve drops Eva back at the station while he makes his way to King's Lynn. He's had a pleasant lunch of fish finger sandwiches with a coffee afterwards. Eva had chosen the same. Steve, who knows the landlady quite well, had asked her to join them for a quick word. He produced the photo of Alecja.

'Oh yes,' she said, 'I saw it on the news last night. Poor girl, she used to come in here with a farmer from somewhere near Outwell way.'

'Jimmy Jackson.' Steve replied and told her of Jimmy's death.

'Oh my God,' the landlady exclaimed, 'and you think she's done it?'

'Not at all, but we do need to talk to her urgently. How often did they come here?'

'Probably once a week, mostly on a weekday. They would arrive around seven, have something to eat and leave before nine. They've also been in for Sunday lunch a few times.'

'And how did they appear to you?'

'Funny you should ask that. Once when they were here, I was talking to one of my regulars who made a remark about gold diggers while he was talking about the girl. I told him I didn't think it was like that at all. She was made up and all that but she wasn't flashy or anything. They looked comfortable with each other. They always talked and I heard them laugh a lot. Not like a lot of couples who come here and either don't say a word to each other or otherwise argue all the time.'

Well, Steve thought, he and Eva also had a pleasant lunch without arguing but then again, they weren't a couple. He thought about Eva; she was a good officer indeed with just the right amount of ambition without being pushy. He was sure she would make an excellent detective. Maybe he should tell her to get on with it. She had joined the police in her late twenties and now, in her mid-thirties, was already older than some of the other detective inspectors on the force.

His thoughts drift to Julia. Last time they had gone to a pub, it had indeed finished with an argument. Thinking about it, lately, they argued every time they spoke. Still, he would ring her again tonight.

Eva also thinks about lunch. She had thoroughly enjoyed the fish finger sandwich. Much better than a plastic slice of bread from the garage. She also enjoyed Steve's company. Although her superior, he had treated her as an equal these last few days. He hadn't minded her butting in and asking questions either, even though she was still a lowly police constable. And she was learning! She carefully noticed how Steve deployed a number of different techniques when talking to people. With the Jacksons, he had been sympathetic, but with the landlady, he let her talk, simply guiding her a bit when necessary, while with the NFU representative, he had been businesslike and to the point. She couldn't wait until tonight; it would be the first time she would be part of a proper interview team questioning a suspect. Well, maybe not a suspect, more like a witness. Still, she couldn't help but smile. This is what she signed up for. Proper detective work, not sorting out drunk teenagers on Norfolk

Street in King's Lynn on a Saturday night.

While Steve and Eva are talking to the Jacksons, DI Woods arrives at Mick Mendham's farm in Leverington. Unlike the previous afternoon, the place is now a hive of activity. A number of men are standing around, smoking, next to a couple of minibuses. When he gets out of the car, two men are leaving the office. One of them shouts:

'Right guys, time to go.'

DI Woods watches as they all pile into the vans and drive away. He walks into the office, where he is greeted by the same woman he spoke to yesterday morning.

'What do you want?' she asks brusquely. 'I told you yesterday: Mick isn't here.'

'Good morning,' replies DI Woods. 'You're right, you did tell me that yesterday, but I'm now asking you again to give me Mick's mobile number.'

'I told you I don't have it,' comes the reply. 'And I don't believe you,' he responds.

'That is your problem. Now leave me alone, I've got work to do.'

'No,' DI Woods says firmly. 'If you don't cooperate, it will definitely become your problem. Deliberately obstructing a police investigation into a murder case almost always ends in a custodial sentence.'

'A murder case!' she exclaims! 'You said nothing about a murder yesterday. Who's been murdered? And why do you want to speak to Mick?'

'None of your business,' DI Woods answers. 'That is for Mr Mendham and me to discuss.'

'I think,' the woman says much more quietly now, 'that if Mick is involved in a murder, it is very much my business. I am Mick's wife.'

16

The port of King's Lynn lies at the mouth of the
Great River Ouse on The Wash. The town was once
a thriving centre of commerce with ships loading
and unloading cargoes of grain, timber and bricks to
and from the continent. During the Middle Ages it
was an important part of the Hanseatic League,
which acted as a sort of unofficial customs union
between the Baltic ports as well as north German
and Dutch cities.

Although its importance has declined over the last
three hundred years, there is still a healthy coming
and going of ships, carrying mainly timber from
Scandinavia and returning with grain from East
Anglia to other northern European sea ports.

Not far from the entrance to the docks complex is
the old fisherman's quarter. Many of the old cottages

have disappeared but some remain, with at the centre a museum, *True's Yard,* celebrating the nautical and social history of the town. The actual town centre is less than a mile away and the road leading to it is scattered with remnants of the town's past importance. Old warehouses, woodyards and of course, a number of pubs. Time was you could hear Scandinavian, Dutch and German accents as a matter of course.

It is in one of these pubs, *The Fisherman's Friend,* that DCI Culverhouse finds himself drinking half a pint of Woodforde's Wherry while considering what his next step should be. He decides to start by walking around the harbour, talking to some of the dockers and taking in the sights and layout of the port complex. Only one ship is moored in the basin today, the *SS Johanna Maria*, a Dutch coaster being loaded with wheat bound for Rotterdam. He quickly concludes there is no way any tractors or other machinery can be loaded onto this vessel. The hold is accessible only via six hatches which are opened to give access to a flexible pipe which at the other end is connected to a large hopper containing the grain.

He talks to some of the workers in and around the port, but no one has seen tractors being loaded onto ships. An older man tells him there are a number of vessels that have the capacity to carry vehicles on deck but that it is years since he has seen any of them in port. Not since the Skoda franchise closed in 1996. What he notices, however, is that away from the main basin there is still the facility for roll-on roll-off ferries to dock. It is directly connected to an old, now overgrown, car park which had once been the site where the new cars, imported from the old Czechoslovakia, were stored until they found their way to dealers across the country. He also notices that some of the weeds growing out of the concrete have recently been flattened and some kind of track has been established.

While walking around the perimeter fence, he is disturbed by a friendly dog whose owner is not far behind.

'Lovely dog,' Steve says by way of a greeting.

'He is, isn't he?' the man replies. 'Don't mind me asking but are you looking for something? It's just, I've never seen you here before,' he adds apologetically.

'No worries,' Steve says and shows him his warrant card, 'as a matter of fact, yes, I'm looking for something, stolen tractors to be precise.'

'In that case, you might have come to the right place. I'm not sure if they are stolen but someone has

114

recently started to park one or two tractors over there.' He points to the far end of the car park.

'They are there for a few days and then they're gone again.'

'You can't remember exactly when?'

'No, but I would say probably two or three times over the last couple of months.'

'How do the tractors get here?'

'I'm not sure,' the man answers. 'I once saw a low-loader truck but whether he dropped them off or was picking them up, I didn't notice.'
He points behind him.

'I live in the flats over there and my kitchen window looks out over this part of the docks. It's such a shame they've let it go to rack and ruin. I tell you what: it wasn't like this when Skoda was here. It was a sad day when they packed up.'

'Thank you,' Steve says, giving the man his card, 'you have been very helpful. Please contact me if you can remember anything else. Or better still, ring me next time you see any more tractors.'

He walks back along the fence until he comes to the entrance. The metal gates are rusty like the rest of the fence but Steve notices the hinges have recently been greased and the gate secured with a brand new padlock. From here, he makes his way back to the Harbour Master's office and introduces himself before enquiring about possible CCTV footage. But no luck. The port's surveillance cameras cover most of the port complex but not the disused car park.

Steve checks his watch, three-thirty, he'd better get back to the station. He's feeling good, the way he feels deep down inside when he is getting closer to solving a case. Rather than taking the bypass, he drives into town and stops at the police station where he speaks to the duty sergeant and asks him to instruct the regular patrols policing the docks to keep a check on the old Skoda car park and ring him if there is any vehicle movement.

When DI Woods reports back later that afternoon, he explains that after he had mentioned the murder investigation Mrs Mendham had become much more cooperative.

'My Mick would never murder anyone,' she had said. 'Rough them up a bit if they deserved it but never murder, not my Mick.'

She told him Mick was on his way back from Harwich via Norwich where he planned to see a client, so she didn't know exactly what time he would arrive home, except that he had promised to be back before seven o'clock as they were planning to go out that night for a meal with friends. She also willingly handed over Mick's mobile number. This had left DI Woods with a bit of a dilemma. He did not want to ring Mick Mendham in front of his wife but at the same time, he knew that the moment he closed the door behind him, she would be on the phone warning Mick. Can't be helped, he decided, she will have told him about my visit yesterday anyway. So he said his goodbyes and made for his car. He dialled Mick's number but it was engaged. He was not surprised. He had tried several times but it was clear Mick had switched his phone off.

'Never mind,' DCS Sutton says, ' did she say where they are meeting their friends tonight?'

'Yes, she told me they were going to the *Carpenters' Arms* for dinner at eight.'

At that moment, DI Starling knocks on the door and introduces the officer in charge of the SOCO team. He explains they have done a thorough search of both the house and the grain store again and have found several pieces of bailing twine similar to that probably used to restrain Jimmy Jackson. They will drop it off at forensics for further testing.

'And we found this,' DI Starling says, producing two plastic evidence bags. The first one is bulging with a great wad of twenty pound notes.

'We estimate there to be roughly forty thousand pounds.'

They turn their attention to the second bag. In it is an envelope containing two thousand pounds, according to DI Starling, again in twenty pound notes. What makes it doubly interesting though, is that on the front of the envelope, instead of the name and address of the intended recipient, it reads: *For Alecja, thank you.*

By four-thirty, everybody, except Eva, is back at the station. Steve is the last to update his colleagues. Before he has finished, Maddy knocks on the door and announces:

'I've got a man downstairs who wants to see DI Woods. He says his name is Mick Mendham.'

After a quick conference on how to deal with this unexpected, but welcome, development, DI Woods and Steve make their way to the foyer where a man in his forties is pacing up and down. When the two detectives introduce themselves, Mick points at DI Woods.

'So you're the fellow who's been harassing my wife?'

'In that case, you must be Mick Mendham,' DI Woods suggests before continuing, 'I've asked her a couple of questions. I wouldn't call that harassment. But thank you for coming in. We can now talk to you directly, so much easier for all of us.'

'Well, I knew you lot wouldn't leave me alone, so as I was passing anyway, I thought I'll pop in. But can we make it quick? I've got a dinner to go to later on and I need a shower and a shave.'

'Let's go somewhere we can sit down,' Steve suggests and they make their way to one of the interview rooms As soon as they are seated, Mick continues:

'I've been away for the last couple of days. What's all this about? Why do you want to see me?'

'You may not have heard,' Steve responds, 'but we are looking into the death of Jimmy Jackson, a farmer from Nordelph.'

Mick is clearly shaken.

'I know Jimmy. Some of my men work for him. My wife mentioned murder. Are you saying Jimmy has been murdered? He wouldn't hurt a fly, why would someone want to kill him? You don't think I've got anything to do with it, do you?'

Steve studies his face. The man appears genuinely surprised and upset by the news.

'I can't answer all your questions but it would be of great help to us if you could answer some of ours.'

Mick nods. 'Go ahead,' he says.

'First of all, can you tell us where you've been for the last three or four days?'

'No problem. I took the ferry from Harwich to the

Hook on Sunday night. I slept on the boat and drove to Groningen in the north, where I stayed with a friend that evening. The next day, I went to an auction in Assen, a town about 25 miles from Groningen. I drove back to the Hook after the auction and took the night ferry back to Harwich. The rest you already know.'

'What kind of auction?' Steve asks.

'Mainly farm machinery,' Mick replies, 'that's my business but not why I went this time. This trip was purely pleasure. Part of the sale was a Zündapp motorbike, used by the German army during the Second World War. That's my hobby, you see,' he adds by way of explanation. 'I collect vintage military vehicles.' He looks at his watch. 'Are we going to be much longer? Only like I said, I've got a dinner to go to.'

'I know,' replies Steve, 'just a few more questions.' He produces the missing poster and without saying anything, places the picture of Alecja on the table before him. Again Mick is clearly genuinely surprised.

'Isn't that the Polish girl, Alice or something like that? She used to work for me at Jimmy's farm. Bloody hell, you don't think she did it do you? I mean she was a mouthy so-and-so but I wouldn't have her down for murder.'

Suddenly his expression changes and he continues as if he is talking to himself.

'Of course, I heard she got together with Jimmy after I sacked her.'

'What do you mean?' DI Woods asks. 'You sacked her? I thought she had been made redundant by Mr Jackson.'

'Same thing really,' Mick responds. 'Jimmy had no work for her anymore, so he rang me to say she was no longer needed. But she is registered on my books, so I suppose it was me who told her Jimmy no longer could employ her. She didn't take it well, called me all sorts. She owed me a fair bit of money in missed rent as well but like I said, she was a mouthy cow, excuse the language, so when I had a chance to get rid of her I did. I haven't employed her since.'

'What do you mean, "get rid of her?"'

'I didn't kill her or anything,' Mick replies, looking anxiously at the detectives. 'I just never gave her another job. It was at the same time that I sold the mobile home she lived in with her sister to a colleague of mine, so I no longer saw her when collecting the rent.'

'Oh yes, you own the mobile home site at Salters Lode.'

'I don't own the site,' Mick replies, 'I rent the land from a retired farmer. I own the mobile homes, well

121

I used to own all of them but like I said, I sold the one the sisters lived in.'

'They are cousins, actually.' DI Woods butts in. 'Whatever you say,' comes the reply. 'Who cares? Can I go now please?' addressing his question directly at Steve.

'Just a couple of quick questions. When and why did you sell that particular mobile home and who did you sell it to?'

'I tell you why,' Mick answers animatedly. 'I know what people think about us gangmasters but I'm telling you I look after my workers. But I take exception when any of them become mouthy and cause me a headache. But I would never throw anybody out on the street, especially not two young women, so when the opportunity came, I sold the home but made it clear that it came with two sitting tenants, so to speak.'

'Very admirable,' Steve replies dryly, 'and who did you sell it to?'

Curly, comes the answer.

'You mean the Dutch guy?' DI Woods interjects.

'He's not Dutch,' Mick replies. 'He's South African, his real name is Derk Pieters but he likes to be called Curly on account of his blond hair. He's a nasty piece of shit if you ask me.'

'So why did you sell the mobile home to him?'

'In my line of work, you can't choose who you deal with. Anyway, I borrowed a couple of thousand from him a while ago. He wanted it back in a hurry but I didn't have the cash at the time, so I offered him the mobile home instead. It's worth more than what I owed him but with no money changing hands, the tax man is none the wiser.'

'You have been very helpful,' Steve says. 'Thanks for coming in. One more question. Where does Mr Pieters live or have you any idea on how to reach him?'

'I don't think he lives anywhere,' Mick replies. 'He once told me that he saw a film, *The Lincoln Lawyer* it was called, where this bloke lives in his car.'
Not quite, thinks Steve who has seen the film, but never mind.

'Anyway, he's got one of those big fuck-off camper trailers, the one where the sides come out to make more space when you're parked up.'

'And where does he keep it?'

'I'm not sure, not around here or I would know. When I've met him he always drives the same car, a black Range Rover.'

17

Eva arrives at the barn conversion around two o'clock. She had rung ahead and Marion had explained that Jack was out but would be back before four or four-thirty at the latest.

'Never mind,' Eva had replied, 'it will give us a chance to talk if you want to.'

Marion welcomes her and leads her into the kitchen. She seems on edge, looking out of the window towards the farm where the SOCO team are busy.

'Haven't they finished yet?' she says. 'I hate it that they are going through all of Jimmy's stuff. It should be private,' she adds by way of explanation.

'I agree,' Eva says, 'it must feel like quite an intrusion but they are professionals and I'm sure they will treat Jimmy's possessions with respect.'

She changes the subject:

'How is it going for you all, how are the kids?'

Talking about the children relaxes Marion a bit.

'They are alright,' she says, 'they're enjoying getting all the attention from my parents.'

'And what about yourselves, you and Jack if you don't mind me calling him that?'

'No it's fine,' she smiles, 'it is his name after all.' She pauses. 'Well, you know what men are like, he doesn't give much away but I think deep inside he is struggling with it all.'

'And what about you?'

'I'm alright. I feel angry more than anything else but I don't know why. Anyway, how is the investigation going?'

'There's not much to say. We've got the whole team on it and extra officers drafted in. But we haven't had a breakthrough yet.'

'So that means the murderer is still out there?' There is not much she can say to that, Eva realises.

'We are doing our best,' she responds, 'these things take time.'

For the fourth time since her arrival, the phone rings. Marion explains that it's yet another journalist.

'I think you should go ex-directory for a while at least,' Eva suggests.

'Good idea,' Marion agrees. 'I'll get on with it immediately,' and walks to the little office next to the front door where she switches her computer on. Not long after four o'clock Eva sees the SOCO van leaving the farm. She tells Marion.

'Let's go,' is the reply.

'Don't you want to wait for your husband?' Eva wonders.

'I'll text him and tell him where we are,' she replies. As Eva is planning to go straight back to Downham from the farm, she takes her own car while Marion drives ahead in her Audi A3.

At the farm, they are greeted by one of the police officers from the Cambridgeshire Force. While they are walking towards the house, he says to Eva:

'I'll be glad when this is over: this must be the most boring job ever.'

Eva sympathises, happy she has not been made part of the surveillance rota. Before they enter the farmhouse, Marion turns to Eva.

'Do you really have to come in? I mean, this is private.'

'I'm sorry,' Eva says. 'I've been told that in situations like this, there has to be supervision and I will have to log anything you remove from the house.'

'Ridiculous,' Marion replies angrily. Eva does not mind: she knows that grief affects people in different ways.

After making their way to the study, Marion sits down at the old-fashioned bureau in the corner. It is the sort of thing you see in auctions going for a song because modern houses aren't big enough for this kind of furniture anymore, however well-made it is.

Eva looks around. The SOCO team have done a brilliant job, especially when you consider there is no obligation for the police or a forensic team to tidy up after a search. But here, you wouldn't guess that only a few hours before, three officers had checked the place over with a toothcomb. It should definitely help in her relationship with the Jacksons, Eva thinks, although just then, she hears a commotion outside. She quickly makes her way to the front door and sees her fellow officer remonstrating with Jack Jackson.

'I bloody well go where I want,' she hears him shout. 'This is my property now.'

'Sorry,' Eva calls out 'I should have told my colleague you were coming, my apologies.'
Still angry, Jack walks into the room to speak to his wife.

'How are you getting on?' he asks by way of a greeting.

'Nothing yet,' she replies. 'It must be here somewhere, I'm sure.'

'I'll have a look in his bedroom,' Jack responds.
What do I do? Eva thinks, I can't keep an eye on both at the same time.

'Can I help?' she suggests.

'No thank you,' Jack responds, 'it's private, financial stuff, you wouldn't know what to look for.' And with that, he runs upstairs but is back ten minutes later.

'Nothing,' he states.

In the meantime, Marion empties most of the bureau. She shows a pile of bank statements to Eva.

'This is part of what we are looking for. Is it okay if we take these?'

Eva has a quick look.

'I can't see any problem with that,' she replies. They leave the house and Eva carefully re-attaches the police tape before walking to her car. Before she gets in, Jack Jackson comes over to her and apologises.

'I'm sorry, I was rude to you and your colleague earlier on. I don't know what came over me; it's all just so horrible.'

'Don't worry,' Eva replies. 'I don't take it personally.'

She gets in her car and drives back to the station, where she arrives in time to see PC Redding and PC Sheldon arrive with Mr Nowak and Mr Kowalski.

Mick Mendham is leaving after handing over Derk Pieters' number.

'Mind you,' he says, 'it's a while since I've spoken to him, so I'm not sure if the number is still in use.'

'Thank you,' Steve replies, walking Mick to his van. 'Let's have a look at this bike.'

Mick opens the back doors.

'There she is,' he says proudly. 'Isn't she wonderful?'

'I have to agree,' Steve says. 'She's a beauty. Enjoy your meal.'

When he walks into the foyer, Maddy tells him DCS Sutton is waiting for him.

'Jack Jackson has been on the phone,' she says when he arrives at her office. 'He's asking how much longer the farm is to be sealed off for. Is there any point in maintaining our presence there? The SOCO team has finished and I heard from the coroner that the body will be released back to the family tomorrow.'

'I agree, but I would like the watch on the mobile home to continue.'

'I'll ask PC Lappinska to ring the Jacksons. Also, we'd better not forget to tell the poor constable he can go home. I will wait for you in my office. Good luck with the interviews.'

Steve finds DI Baker and Eva in the kitchen. Together they make their way to the interview room, where Mr Kowalski is waiting for them.

'Where is Mr Nowak?' he wants to know.

'We'll see him separately,' is the reply.

'But he doesn't speak good English.'

'Don't worry,' DI Baker smiles, 'we'll deal with that.'

Eva has been asked to take notes. Steve has told her to feel free to indicate if she wants to ask a supplementary question. As it is, the interview doesn't throw up anything they don't already know. Mr Kowalski explains they have worked for Mick Mendham for around five years, the last two at Jimmy Jackson's farm. He and Mr Nowak have become friends, although they'd never met before they came to England. Mick Mendham is a good boss and so was Jimmy Jackson. They liked him but he wouldn't listen to advice, he was a bit careless.

'What do you mean?' Steve asks.

'Well, when he got his new tractor after the other one was stolen, he was careful for about the first few weeks. He would lock the tractor and the barn doors every night and take the keys with him inside the house. But before long he went back to the old system of leaving the keys in the lean-to. I warned him but he laughed and said he didn't think the thieves would come back a second time.'

'Is there anything you can remember from the last

couple of days before he was killed?' Steve asks.

'Did he have any visitors or did you see anything else out of the ordinary?'

'I don't think so. Jack, his son, popped in a few times and so did Jack's wife. But they often did. Oh, and Mick Mendham came to see us at home on the Sunday before. He came to collect the rent but said he had spoken to Jimmy and that everything was okay as far as the job was going.'

'Did he normally collect the rent on a Sunday?'

'Not always,' is the reply. 'The rent is due on Fridays but Mick comes any time during the weekend. Depending on when he is in the area, I suppose. He said he was on his way to Harwich.'

'What time was that?'

'Around six o'clock I think, maybe a bit later.'

'Thanks. I now want to ask you about Curly. What can you tell us about him?'

'From what I hear, he's not a good man,' Mr Kowalski replies. 'I have never met him myself but some of our friends work for him and they don't like him. They say he shouts a lot and doesn't always pay on time.'

'Thank you.' Steve turns to DI Baker and Eva, who both shake their heads. 'No more questions. You are free to go. We will give you a lift back to Salters Lode once we have finished with Mr Nowak.'

They have a quick break, while Eva rings the Jacksons, after which they move to the room next door where Mr Nowak is waiting.

'Sorry to have kept you,' Steve says while he introduces DI Baker. 'And Eva of course, you've already met,' inviting her to translate.

The moment she starts speaking in Polish a transformation takes place in Mr Nowak. Gone is the sullen expression. Instead, he gets up and starts speaking rapidly, addressing Eva directly with a series of questions, finishing with pointing his finger directly at her face. She remains calm throughout. Just when Steve is about to interfere he stops and sits down again.

'What was all that?'

'He wants to know why he is here and how long we are keeping him. He insists he has done nothing wrong and says we are victimising him because he's foreign. He's going to walk out unless he is satisfied with what we have to say.'

'Tell him we are here to ask him questions, not the other way round. He won't be detained a moment longer than necessary. He is not under arrest and if he wants to walk out, he can do so, but it is four miles to Salters Lode and it has started to rain. If he cooperates, he'll be out of here in no time and get a lift back.'

Eva translates and Steve finishes by saying:

'Tell him he is not here because he is foreign but because he was found at a murder scene.'

Mr Nowak appears to calm down. Steve thinks he can actually hear a muffled 'sorry' coming from the man's mouth. They go through the same questions they've discussed with Mr Kowalski but it is soon clear Mr Nowak has little to add. That is until they come to Curly.

'I don't know where he lives,' says Mr Nowak, 'but I see him sometimes.'

Eva translates and instinctively asks 'Where?'

'I cannot tell you but I'll tell them,' he replies, pointing at the two male detectives. Eva explains the conversation to the others.

'I can nip out for a minute,' she suggests.

'I don't like it,' Steve responds, 'but if you don't mind?'

Eva leaves the room. Steve turns to Mr Nowak.

'Well,' he says, 'why all the secrecy, where do you see Mr Curly?'

'In the brothel in Peterborough,' is the embarrassed reply.

'So, where are we?'

DCS Sutton, Steve, DI Starling and DI Baker are sitting around the table in the incident room. DI

133

Woods is dropping Mr Nowak and Mr Kowalski off in Salters Lode before driving to Jimmy Jackson's farm to give the good news to the constable on duty and remove the police tape. DCS Sutton is standing in front of a brand new whiteboard, marker pen in hand. She explains she decided to do away with the flipcharts and had ordered the new board a couple of weeks ago. By chance, it had arrived earlier that day.

'One day,' she adds with a generous dose of sarcasm in her voice, 'we might even have an interactive whiteboard.'

It irritates her that the government invests millions in equipping schools, even nurseries for four-year-olds, with the latest technology, but the police force is yet again the poor relation.

Like the previous night, they all contribute their thoughts and ideas but Steve soon realises it doesn't amount to much.

'What worries me,' he says, 'is that I think we are making some progress as far as solving Jimmy Jackson's death. But we seem to be absolutely not any nearer finding Ms Tobinska. And when I think of all the blood she lost, I fear the worst.'

'I agree,' DI Starling concurs. 'We've established there is a connection between the two but at the same time, these are two different investigations, if you know what I mean. To put it bluntly, one person is dead but the other, we hope, is still alive. So she must be our priority.'

'Okay,' DI Baker says, 'but we also agree Ms Tobinska's disappearance is almost certainly connected with Mr Jackson's death. If we could solve who shot him, we might get closer to the whereabouts of Ms Tobinska.'

They all look at DCS Sutton.

'I think we are going around in circles. Let's get back to basics. Where are we on motive?'

'I'm sure,' Steve says, 'it is almost certainly something to do with money and the cash found in the glove compartment of Jimmy's car should give us a clue but at the moment, I can't for the life of me think of what it could be.'

'Except of course, that it establishes definite proof, if we needed it, that Jimmy Jackson and Alecja were involved,' DI Starling points out.

'What if,' interjects DCS Sutton, 'Ms Tobinska was party to the murder? I know we think she wouldn't have the strength to carry it out by herself but what if she was an accomplice or even the instigator? She might have somehow faked the blood in her kitchen to put us off the scent and got herself across the Channel back to Poland.'

'But why would she do that?' Steve replies. 'Jimmy was clearly planning to give her money, so why kill him?'

'But that was only two thousand pounds, what if she knew about the rest and wanted all of it?' DI Baker says. 'And where did the money come from? Do you think it might be worth it to have PC Sheldon, with his number skills, go through Mr Jackson's accounts and see whether that gives us some idea?'

They all agree. At least it's something concrete to focus on tomorrow morning.

DCS Sutton turns to Steve.

'Where does Mick Mendham fit in?'

'I'm not sure,' Steve says. 'He wasn't what I expected him to be. He was actually quite cooperative but I do have the feeling he is connected somehow. I am planning some further enquiries tomorrow about his movements in the Netherlands.'

'Could he have threatened Mr Jackson before he left?' DI Baker asks. 'Didn't you say he most likely saw Jimmy on Sunday evening before he drove to Harwich? Could he have shot him on Sunday night, only for the body to be found on Monday morning?'

'Unlikely,' Steve replies. 'I've checked the pathologist's report. She is certain he had his heart attack around the same time he was shot and this would have occurred between two and six hours before the body was found. Mick Mendham took the eleven o'clock night ferry from Harwich, so unless our pathologist is mistaken, which is unlikely, and Mr Mendham is lying, that scenario doesn't work.

And Mr Mendham is smart enough to realise I will check his presence on the ferry and his other comings and goings as soon as the offices in Harwich open tomorrow morning.'

'Aren't they open now?'

'Some are, but the person with the authority to sanction the release of this data is not in the office until tomorrow morning.'

While he is talking, he is racking his brain. Something about Mick Mendham doesn't add up. But what is it?

18

The next time Alecja wakes up, she feels different. Her head is surprisingly clear but she is conscious of a gnawing desire in her mouth and stomach. Suddenly she recognises the feeling. It is the same as when she tried to give up smoking once. In the end, she had given in. Oh, how she could do with a cigarette now. She feels inside her pocket. Her phone is gone but to her surprise, she finds a nearly full packet of cigarettes. And there on the table, next to the oil lamp, is a box of matches. She feels as if she's won the lottery. But when she lights the cigarette and inhales the first drag, she almost falls back onto the bed, so strong is the effect the tobacco has on her. She eats another banana and wonders what is happening to her. After a little while, the initial shock of having the first dose of nicotine in several days becomes less strong and smoking now helps her to concentrate. She lights another one. She has no idea why she is here, surely not for the couple of hundred quid she owes Curly. It must be something else. She stretches her brain. If only Jimmy was here. It feels so long ago that they were sitting next to the blazing fire in the Carpenters' Arms eating their roast beef. No, she doesn't know why she is here but she does know she has to get out. She tries to stand up and gingerly makes her way around the walls of the small building. There are quite a few windows but they are all high up and there is no way she can reach them. Apart from the front door, there are two, quite rickety-looking, double doors at the back of the building. One of them has a broken panel of wood so she can see outside. She peers through the hole and looks out onto a small river. Across the bank, in the distance, are some large greenhouses. By now, she is tired and so finds her way back to the bed and lies down. She makes a plan. When the man comes back, she will pretend she is still very weak. She has to build up her strength and then make her escape. She is sure forcing the other planks in the back door won't be a problem but she needs to get stronger first. Just then, she hears a car. When the man comes inside, she pretends to be asleep. He talks quietly.

'Ah good, you've eaten some more.'
He leans over her.

'But you're still comatose, I see. Maybe only half a

dose today.'

He produces a syringe. Alecja doesn't move as yet
again the warming fluid enters her body.

19

Steve walks to his car. He feels a little uneasy but can't work out why. He's sure it's got something to do with Mick Mendham but he can't put his finger on it. He actually quite liked Mick. A little rough and inappropriate with his language, perhaps, but nothing like the bully he'd expected. And it is clear his workers like him. Or are they too scared to say anything in case it gets back to Mick?

He sighs, what a life most of them have, living in squalid conditions, at the mercy of gangmasters and disliked by the locals. Not a good combination. Still, several came, settled and before long integrated. He'd even heard the story of a Lithuanian woman who married an English guy from Wisbech. She and her husband were now actually campaigning in favour of Brexit. Unbelievable, Steve thinks. He stays out of politics on the whole but his colleagues are clear where he stands on Brexit. He is also aware he definitely is in a minority in this part of the country.

His mood has not improved by the time he arrives home on the new estate just off the Lynn Road on the north-west of town. He remembers he was planning to ring Julia tonight but at the same time realises how hungry he is. It's getting late and he does not feel like cooking from scratch. He turns the car around and makes his way towards the High Street and parks outside an Indian restaurant. A second takeaway in two days will do fine.

The spring rain, which had been falling earlier, has changed into a miserable drizzle and Steve hurries inside. He immediately feels surrounded by the pleasant embrace of spices, warmth and distant mood music. He makes his way through the almost empty restaurant to the back, where they have some seats reserved for takeaway customers.

As soon as he sits down, he hears a voice next to him say:

'Great minds think alike.'

He half turns and finds himself looking at the smiling face of Eva Lappinska.

'They do indeed,' he says. 'What are you doing here?'

Realising the stupidity of his question, he jokes:

'Making inquiries, I suppose.'

'Of course,' she replies, 'and I have heard the Lamb Shashlik Bhuna is especially good here.'

'In that case, I shall order the same.'

Eva's turn is next and she gets up to walk to the till and place her order. Steve instinctively stands up himself and joins her.

'I'll have a Lamb Shashlik Bhuna with pilau rice and garlic naan bread, please,' he hears her say.

'I'll have the same,' Steve says.

The waiter stares at them, slightly puzzled.

'Are you together? Eat-in or takeaway?'

Steve turns to Eva.

'What do you think?'

'I don't mind,' she replies, 'beats walking home through the drizzle.'

'Eat in please,' Steve addresses the waiter, 'and oh, can I have a bottle of Tiger beer please?'

He turns to Eva.

'What about you?'

'I'll have some mineral water, thank you.'

They are seated by the waiter at a table near the window, which gives them a perfect view of the empty High Street where every now and then, car lights reflect the wet surface of the tarmac. They are both quiet, waiting for the waiter to return with some poppadoms. Steve wonders if Eva regrets saying yes to a shared meal on the spur of the moment.

To rescue the situation he says:

'I'm glad I caught you: there's a couple of things I

want to ask you.'

He glances around. There is nobody on the other tables and only the occasional customer coming through the front door making their way to the takeaway counter. He continues:

'When we were in the interview this afternoon, Mr Nowak pointed at you and said something directly to you. I don't speak Polish but it didn't sound pleasant. Am I right to think you didn't translate that bit?'

Was it his impression or did she blush just a little bit.

'I'm sorry,' she says. 'I didn't think it was important.'

'Come on,' says Steve, 'let's have it out, what was it?'

'Mr Nowak was angry finding out I could speak Polish and felt I had tricked him and Mr Kowalski when we interviewed them at home yesterday.'

'Was that it?' Steve replies, 'Are you sure?'

'No, he did get himself badly worked up and started calling me names.'

'What kind of names?'

'He called me a traitor and a whore,' she says quietly.

The waiter arrives with their snacks, so for a minute, they are quiet. Steve is about to say something when Eva asks:

'Tell me if I am out of order or if you can't answer this, but what did he say to you when I left the room?'

'You're not out of order and I was going to tell you anyway. Mr Nowak said he occasional saw our Mr Pieters in a brothel in Peterborough.'

At this moment his phone rings, shit, it's Julia! He turns the volume down a little and returns the phone to his pocket. A minute later, he hears the familiar sound of an incoming text message. He takes his phone out again and reads what Julia has written. It simply says, *"I don't know why I bother."*

Eva looks at him. 'Important?'

'No, nothing,' Steve replies.

The food arrives and for the next fifteen minutes, they are both busy eating the house speciality, which, they agree, is indeed a culinary delight. When they finish the waiter arrives with the dessert menu.

'Nothing for me,' Eva says.

'Nor me,' Steve agrees, 'but I would like a coffee.'

'And you madam?'

'Do you do decaff?' Eva asks.

'Of course,' the waiter replies.

'Thank you, that is what I'll have.' Eva hands back the menus.

'Earlier on, you said there were a couple of things you wanted to ask me. What was the other thing?'

'Oh yes, listen, this is off the record and probably none of my business but I wondered if you had thought about transferring to CID at all?'

'Why do you ask?' Eva responds.

'Because I think you would be good at it. Earlier this afternoon, with Mr Nowak insulting you, you stayed calm and professional throughout. From the little I've seen, you've got all the right qualities.'

'It's kind of you to say so. I think about it sometimes but I'm not sure.'

'Well,' Steve says, 'when you've made up your mind let me know and I'll try and give you all the support you might need. And not only me, I'm sure DCS Sutton will do the same.'

They finish their coffees and make moves to leave. The bill arrives and Steve doesn't argue when Eva insists on paying her share. They step outside, where it is now dry.

'Can I give you a lift?' Steve offers. 'You said you came on foot.'

'Thank you,' Eva replies, 'but I think I can do with some fresh air so I can walk off a few calories. See you tomorrow, goodbye.'

And off she is, around the corner, making her way down Bridge Street to the new development near the station where she had bought a small terraced house only a month before.

Steve arrives home, pours himself a whiskey and makes for his favourite armchair in the garden room. They called it a conservatory when they had it build shortly after buying the house four years ago but it is much more like a proper room. It is the ideal place to sit in the evening admiring the spectacular Fenland sunsets, but no such joy tonight because by the time he sits down, it has been dark for at least three hours. He gets his phone out.

Should he ring Julia? Too late, she'll be in bed. He decides to text instead. "*Sorry about tonight, got called away, only just got back.*" It is a lie but what else is he going to say? "*Sorry, but I couldn't talk because I was having dinner with an attractive colleague of mine.*" That wouldn't have gone down too well either. It's all a mess, he decides, feeling guilty and somewhat deflated. Still, he enjoyed spending the evening with Eva.

He decides on one more whiskey, leans back and selects Richard Thompson's *1952 Vincent Black Lighting* from his Spotify playlist. It turns his thoughts to Mick Mendham and his motorbike. Maybe he should restore his father's old BSA, which is gathering dust in a shed on the farm. He has an idea. If Julia doesn't come, he'll go and see his dad this weekend. He turns off the lights and makes his way to bed. Just before he falls asleep, his thoughts turn back to Eva, Was it his imagination or had her hand touched his arm ever so slightly when she said goodbye?

Eva is in her kitchen making herself a hot chocolate. She's enjoyed the way the evening unexpectedly turned out. She's had a pleasant few hours in good company rather than eating her takeaway on her own in front of the telly. Fair enough, they'd only talked about work but still, better than *Bake Off*, for sure. But why had she held back when Steve suggested her joining CID? It was all she wanted to do. Why didn't she admit it to him? No point worrying about it now she decides. She's had a nice evening. Let's leave it at that. She makes her way to bed.

But when she lies down, she can't get his face out of her head. *'Stop it!'* she tells herself, *'You're done with men. Remember what happened last time.'* Her mind wanders back to the awful days seven years ago when she found out that her fiancé had been cheating on her. They'd only just moved in together and she was so devastated by the blow that it had taken her over a year to regain some resemblance of her old self. It was at this time that she handed in her notice at the law firm where she had worked since leaving university and joined the police force.

Her thoughts drift slowly back to the present. Yes,

she tells herself, that time seven years ago was awful but none of it had been Steve's fault. She turns around, hugs her pillow, and once more recalls Steve's face. She admits to herself that ever since she first met him, she's liked him.

But, after tonight, she likes him just a little bit more.

THURSDAY

20

When Steve arrives at the station the next morning, he finds a message from DCS Sutton that she has been called to attend a meeting at Norfolk Police Headquarters in Wymondham. In the incident room, DI Starling and DI Baker are already waiting for him.

'What's the plan, boss?' Both detectives look at him expectantly.

'I think it's best,' he suggests, 'that we start tidying up some loose ends. DI Starling, I'd like you to go back to Lena and start putting some pressure on her. I'm sure she knows, or maybe suspects, more than she lets on. Feel free to stress the danger we think her cousin is in after Jimmy's death. Don't be afraid to explain that we think that Ms Tobinska was actually involved in the murder of Mr Jackson. See how she reacts. Take PC Redding with you to take notes.'

'No problem,' DS Starling replies, 'I was going to suggest the same thing myself. Great minds think alike.'

Where have I heard that before recently? Steve wonders before smiling to himself. Of course, last night at the restaurant. He turns to DI Baker:

'John, I would like you to go and visit the Jacksons and ask them to hand over Jimmy's banking history for us to examine. They don't know about the money we found but I think we are all agreed that keeping £40,000.00 cash in a glove compartment of your car is not usual. Check if he has recently withdrawn large sums of money and see if you can spot any irregularities. Take PC Lappinska with you. She has met the family and hopefully, they trust her enough by now to allow us a look at Jimmy's accounts. By the way, don't forget to sign for anything you take out of the house. While you and Eva are at the Jacksons, I will ask PC Sheldon to check with the ferry company regarding Mick Mendham's travel arrangements.'

That is more or less it, Steve decides. Earlier, he had spoken to DI Woods and asked him to go to Wisbech on his way to Downham.

'Visit the nightclub on the barge again,' he suggested, 'and try to get an address and phone number for the bouncer out of the manager. If he is difficult, remind him this is now a murder investigation.'

The six extra police constables have been told to report back to their home base but be ready to be deployed again at short notice, should the need arise.

And that is everyone sorted for a while, Steve thinks to himself while making a cup of coffee in the kitchen. It worries him, though, that in spite of all the activity they are not any further with discovering Ms Tobinska's whereabouts. She seems to have disappeared from the face of the earth. It's one thing if she doesn't want to be found but what if she is wounded somewhere, crying out for help? He shudders but tells himself if that was the case, someone, at some point, would have seen or heard something. He walks to his office, picks up the phone and rings Mick Mendham.

'What now?' Mick asks as he picks up the phone.

'Morning Mick,' Steve replies. 'Did you have a nice meal last night?'

'As a matter of fact, I did,' comes the reply. 'But to be honest, I don't think it's any of your business.'

'My my, you're a bit tetchy this morning. And here I was just making a friendly call.'

'Well, get on with it then,' Mick says.

'Okay, I'll come straight to the point.' He smiles to himself. 'You don't happen to have a manual for a 1956 BSA Bantam D3 do you?'

'I do, as a matter of fact.'

Mick sounds relieved.

'I've got the *Haynes 1948 - 1967* manual; why?'
Steve explains about his father's old motorbike and before long, the two of them are engaged in a friendly conversation about the ups and downs of motorcycle restoration. When they finish Mick says, half-jokingly:

'I can't believe that's all you rang about.'

'It isn't,' Steve replies. 'Why didn't you tell me you went to see Jimmy on your way to Harwich the night before he died?'

Just after he has finished his call with Mick Mendham, Maddy knocks on the door.

'I thought you'd want to see this straight away,' she says and puts a letter on Steve's desk. It is addressed *"To the officer in charge of Mr J Jackson's investigation."*
He opens the letter. It is from a firm of solicitors in Ely. It reads:

Dear Sir/Madam

It has come to our attention that the death of our client Mr J Jackson, residing at Wood View Farm, Silt Road, Nordelph is being investigated by the Fenland Police Force. It is for this reason we wish to inform you that Mr Jackson made an appointment to see us a few days before his death as he was planning to amend his will. The appointment was scheduled for yesterday morning. When he failed to turn up at the agreed time, we made some enquiries and learnt about his unfortunate death and your interest in the matter. Whether or not his appointment with us is relevant to your investigation is of course, for you to decide.

Do not hesitate to contact me if our firm can be of any help in this matter.

Signed

Ms B Fowler, Partner

Steve puts the letter down. Now that is interesting, he says to himself, but decides to wait until DCS Sutton is back before responding. There's a clock on his wall. Still an hour to go before lunch. He opens his laptop and finds the email address for the police station in Assen, the Dutch town where Mick Mendham said he'd been to the auction and bought his motorbike. No harm in checking a few more facts.

DI Starling, Lena and PC Redding are having coffee in a café overlooking the Tuesday Market Place in King's Lynn. DI Starling has told Lena she needs to have a frank conversation without withholding any information.

'And it's up to you,' she continues, 'we can do it here in King's Lynn or back at the station.'

'We talk here,' Lena says. 'I will answer all your questions and tell you everything I know. All I want is for my cousin to be safe.'

'Okay,' DI Starling replies. 'Did you know she was having a relationship with Mr Jackson?'

'I once saw them together, he dropped her off, but when I asked her, she said, no, of course not, he is far too old for me. Just some business.'

'What kind of business?'

'I asked but she wouldn't tell me. All she said is that it had something to do with Mick Mendham and the farm. I didn't believe her but she would not say anything else.'

'What about Mick Mendham?'

'He was okay with me but I think Alecja annoyed him; I'm not sure why. After he sold our mobile home to Curly, I only ever saw him when he came to the site to collect rent from the other people. I never talked to him again.'

'Tell me about Curly?'

155

'I don't know much about him. He is rough and aggressive. Alecja hates him. They always argue about rent and work.'

'Last time, you mentioned Curly threatening Alecja.'

'Oh yes, he always says things like, if you don't pay, I'll get my money somehow and suggesting she goes and works in a brothel in Peterborough.'

'You told us Alecja was excited about something on the day she disappeared and she was going to tell you later that night. Do you have any idea what it was?'

'No, but it will have something to do with getting money. She hates being poor. The whole reason she came to England was to earn more money than she could in Poland.'

'Isn't that the same for all immigrants?'

'Not for me,' Lena replies. 'I liked my job in Poland but I always loved learning about England and I wanted to see it for myself. If someone had told me how badly we would be treated, especially now with Brexit, I would never have come. If it wasn't for Alecja, I would have gone home a long time ago.'

'What do you mean, if it wasn't for Alecja?'

'I sort of feel responsible for her. She always gets into trouble, nothing serious most of the time, but she can be impulsive. She trusts people too quickly

and gets hurt because they turn out to be bastards.'
She blushes.

'Sorry,' she adds.

'A few more questions. Do you think Alecja disappeared of her own accord?'

'Why would she do that?'

'Could she have been part of the plan to attack Mr Jackson? Could she now be scared, either of the people who did it or simply because she is worried about being caught by the police?'
Lena starts crying but eventually she speaks.

'I don't want to say this but in my heart, I have thought the same thing. But why or how?'
DI Starling takes Lena's hands and looks her straight in the eye.

'Have you heard anything, *anything at all,* from your family or other Polish people here in England that Alecja might be back in Poland?'

'I have heard nothing,' she says. 'I think Alecja would be too proud to go back home with nothing. And anyway, how could she go back? I told you before, Curly has our passports!'

When DI Baker and PC Lappinska arrive at the Jackson's house, they are greeted by Marion in the drive.

'I was on my way out,' she says, 'will it take long?'

DI Baker explains the purpose of the visit. Marion gives him an angry look.

'Why do you want to waste your time on looking at his bank account? Why aren't you out there trying to find who killed poor Jimmy?'
She turns away from them and gets her phone out before breaking out in a long tirade to the person on the other end of the line. Finally, she calms down. She turns around, holding her phone up in the air.

'Jack is asking whether you'll get a warrant if we don't hand them over now?'

'Almost certainly,' DI Baker replies, loudly so Jack can hear the answer. Marion puts the phone back to her ear and listens for a few minutes before addressing John and Eva.

'Jack says take what you need but bring it back as soon as you are finished with it. By the way, I'm taking photos of every scrap of paper you remove.'
She makes another quick call and together, they enter the house where the two police officers are asked to sit down in a small snug adjoining the study. Eva realises she'd not noticed this room before.

While Marion busies herself sorting through papers and taking photographs, Eva surveys the small room. Someone in the family is obviously musical as there are two guitars, a violin and a mandolin hanging on one of the walls.

'I love music,' she remarks to DI Baker. 'Look at these beauties,' pointing to the wall.

'Do you play?' Marion asks from the other room. Her voice sounds friendlier now.

'Only a little piano,' Eva replies, 'but I'd like to get better.'

'You should talk to Jack,' Marion suggests, 'he's mad about music. He plays guitar and piano. The violin and mandolin are meant for the kids but they take little interest. Actually, Jack recently bought a second-hand baby grand.'

'That sounds great!' Eva replies, relieved Marion appears less stressed now.

After having an excellent cappuccino with cake and a cigarette on the Market Square in Wisbech, DI Woods makes his way to the quay where the nightclub is based. It appears deserted, which doesn't surprise him at this time of the morning, but he knocks all the same. No reply. He knocks again but this time shouts, 'Police.' He hears movement inside and a lock turning and is greeted with a friendly:

'What the fuck do you want, don't you know what time it is?'

The manager is only partly dressed and clearly not pleased at being woken this early.

'Sorry,' DI Woods replies, 'I won't keep you long. Can I have the phone number and the address for your doorman Kacper, please?'

'I told your lot yesterday I don't know,' is the reply. 'You'll have to wait until tomorrow night: he'll be here then.'

He starts closing the door but DI Woods steps forward and prevents it from being shut.

'I don't believe you,' he says.

'You believe whatever you want,' is the comeback.

'You might want to tell that to my boss. Come on, get your clothes on. We're going down to the station,' before adding, 'the Downham Police Station, not the Wisbech one.'

'For fuck's sake. What's the hurry?'

'You are obstructing a murder investigation by withholding information.'

'Murder?'

The man is suddenly wide awake.

'You didn't say anything about murder. I thought it was about a missing woman and now you tell me she's been murdered? Wait here. I'll get you the address.'

DI Woods smiles to himself; a little threat often pays off. Okay, so he never said the girl had been murdered but if that's what it takes to get him to cooperate, who is he to argue?

Ten minutes later, he crosses a large roundabout before following the river for a few minutes. He turns into a crescent of beautiful Georgian terraces before passing the town's museum and making for his car. The address he's been given is not in Wisbech itself but in Elm, a village on the edge of town. He parks in the car park of a Chinese restaurant and walks a hundred metres or so before he gets to the right house. He knocks on the door, which is opened immediately by a tall man wearing nothing but a pair of shorts and trainers. He's sweating and it's obvious he's in the middle of a workout.

'Yes?'

DI Woods explains the purpose of his visit.

'Come in, that is a bad thing happening, the girl disappearing. Sorry, my English is not good.'

'A lot better than my Polish,' replies DI Woods.

'How can I help? I do not know the girl.'

DI Woods produces the poster.

'But you have seen her before, haven't you?' he says, pointing at the picture of Alecja.

'Oh yes. Nice girl but always come on her own.'

'Did you ever see her leave with anyone?'

'Let me think, no, I cannot remember. Give me your number; if I remember I will ring you.'

'Thank you,' DI Woods says. 'You've been very helpful.'

'One more thing. Do you know a man called Curly?'

'Yes! I remember now,' Kacper replies enthusiastically. 'She was outside having a cigarette and Curly walked past. They talked for a minute and then she started shouting at him and he left.'

'When was this?'

'I think about two weeks ago, maybe more. I'll try and remember.'

'How well do you know Curly? Is he a regular?'

'He not come often. Good thing, when he comes other customer leave. They all scared of him.'

'Any idea where he lives?'

'I do not know where his house is but he is every night in his brothel in Peterborough. I have worked for him there. I show you where it is.'

He gets out his phone, brings up Google Earth and points at a shopfront.

'The brothel is upstairs,' he says. 'Don't tell him I told you. I'm not scared, but don't tell him I told you.'

PC Sheldon is busy sorting out the paperwork given to him by DI Baker. Eva is helping him. He admits to himself he likes this kind of challenge. He has sorted the financial records into relevant piles, such as Savings Account, Current Account, ISAs and Building Society Account. He and Eva painstakingly examine every transaction of more than £1,000.00 carried out over the last six months. It takes them until three o'clock after which he reports they have found nothing unusual.

'I'm sorry,' he apologises to Steve and DCS Sutton.

'No excuses needed,' Sarah says. 'At least we now know the £40,000.00 did not come from his own accounts and neither did the money he had earmarked to give to Ms Tobinska. Well done, thank you. Could you please write up your report and highlight every occasion larger sums of money are deposited or withdrawn, with the relevant dates of course? Thank you, good work.'

PC Sheldon leaves the room but Eva stays behind. This is the first time she has seen Steve today!

'I was thinking,' she starts, 'Marion Jackson was not happy this morning. Now that we've found nothing wrong, should I go and tell her and try and make amends? They've got enough problems as it is without falling out with us.'

Steve is about to say something but Sarah interrupts,

'Excellent idea, PC Lappinska. You go ahead but can you make sure you are back at the station before six-thirty? I'd like a little chat.'

Eva nods, says goodbye and leaves the room without looking at Steve. Has she done something wrong? Did someone complain about the two of them being in the restaurant last night? *Oh my God,* she suddenly remembers, *Not only the restaurant but also the pub at lunchtime! You could read a lot into that if you wanted to.*

She gets in her car and drives towards Nordelph. She's a bit calmer now. *'Nothing happened,'* she tells herself. Some in the police force might still frown on relationships between the ranks but for God's sake, this is the 21st century, not the Middle Ages. And like she told herself, *'nothing happened!'*

Apart from Sergeant Newman and the three police constables, the rest of the team are meeting in the incident room. DCS Sutton explains she was told by the Deputy Chief Constable that unless there are sudden important developments which warrant more manpower, the six extra constables from Norfolk and Cambridgeshire are to rejoin their home forces. Steve explains that has already happened. Fenland Police can keep PCs Sheldon, Redding and Lappinska but their deployment is to be carefully monitored and reviewed on a daily basis. Fair enough, Steve thinks. Without further leads, there is no need for the extra officers. And they have precious few leads to follow up.

He informs the others that Dutch police have got back to him stating that according to the paperwork from the auctioneers, it was indeed Mick Mendham who bought the motorbike. Also, PC Sheldon has established with the Stena Line Ferry Company that Mr Mendham travelled on the overnight sailing. In other words, his alibi seems to check out. Steve relays the last bit of his phone conversation with Mick to the others. When he had asked why Mick had failed to mention he had seen Jimmy Jackson the day before he was found dead, the man had replied:

'What would you have done? You visit someone and they are found murdered the next day, surely you'd be brought in as a suspect straight away. Anyway, I had nothing to do with Jimmy's murder, you know that.'

Steve had not commented, but instead asked:

'What was the purpose of your visit to Mr Jackson that evening?'

'More like late afternoon,' Mick had replied. 'Every now and then, I visit my farmers to see if they are happy with the workers I've supplied. As I was driving to Harwich anyway, it was only a few miles out of my way and I had a bit of time to kill. Better having a chat with Jimmy than sitting in a queue on the docks at Harwich for an hour.'

'What was Mr Jackson's mood like?' Steve had asked.

'Interesting you ask that,' Mick had replied. 'He was in a great mood, more animated than I've ever seen him before. I asked him if he'd won the lottery.'

"Something like that," he'd replied before apologising to Mick that he needed to leave, explaining he had been invited for Sunday dinner by his daughter-in-law.

DCS Sutton spoke to the solicitors in Ely who, according to her, had little to add to the letter they had sent. They did not know what changes to his will Mr Jackson was planning. They explained they had been the family solicitor for the Jacksons for a long time. The last time they actually had direct dealings with Jimmy had been after the death of his wife and the sorting out of her estate. It had all gone smoothly and they had nothing further to add.

One interesting point is made by DI Baker. He wonders if there is any possibility of linking the black four-by-four Eva saw coming out of Jimmy Jackson's drive to any of the people they discussed so far. But going through the list of people linked to both Alecja and Jimmy, it becomes clear almost everyone drives this kind of vehicle. According to Mick Mendham, Derk Pieters has one. So does Mick himself. Steve has seen one in Jack Jackson's garage. Dr Walker arrived in one at the grain store.

'What,' Steve laughs, looking at his colleague, 'even DI Woods here drives one and we are not suspecting him, are we?'

This only leaves the discovery of the possible whereabouts of Curly, or Derk Pieters as they now know he is called, to be investigated. It is decided Steve and DI Woods will go to Peterborough in the hope Pieters is at his usual hangout as described by doorman Kacper in his conversation with DI Woods.

While Steve is getting ready to go to Peterborough DCS Sutton joins him in his office.

'I really hope this is going to lead to something,' she confides. 'I'm not sure where to go next if it doesn't.'

'Well,' Steve replies, 'let's hope Curly is there and in a talkative mood.'

'Sorry I didn't consult you but just so you know, I've called another quick press conference for tonight. I'm doing it from my office via Zoom. I think it's important we keep the story in the public eye.'

'I agree. At this stage, we might as well, because as it is, we are getting nowhere fast.'

'Before you go,' Sarah continues, 'I'm meeting with PC Lappinska later on. I'm thinking of suggesting she might want to apply to be transferred to CID. I had a look at the *Fast Track* programme last night.

PC Lappinska ticks all the boxes. I think she would make an excellent detective. What do you think?'
Steve smiles to himself.

'Great minds think alike,' he says while putting on his jacket.

21

When Alecja next wakes, she can't work out what time of day it is, let alone which day of the week. But she can see the sun streaming in through the windows. She eats another banana, drinks some water and lights a cigarette. She is feeling much better. She realises she is being drugged but having only received half a dose last time has given her a better night's sleep without affecting the rest of her body too much. She walks around the room. Yes, she is still tired but she's got to get out of here as soon as possible. She finds an old bit of metal and uses it to prise away three of the planks in the door, enough to get through she thinks, but the exercise has exhausted her. She puts the wood back as best she can and decides to get some rest. After about an hour, she eats the rest of the food, drinks the last of the water and has another cigarette. She listens carefully but can't hear a car. She gets through the opening in the door without any problem but now finds herself on a slippery metal ledge just above the water. 'I should swim to the other side and make for the greenhouses,' she thinks, there will be people there.' But she decides against it. She's not sure she has the strength to make it to the other side of the river. Instead, she carefully shuffles along the ledge until she gets to the corner and reaches dry land. She rests for a while. She continues on a rough farm track leading from the front of the building to a road, some 300 metres away. She can hear a tractor in the distance. I must get to the road, she tells herself. Determined, she sets off, resting every now and then, and trying to hide behind the willows growing on one side of the track as much as possible. Finally, she makes it to the road. She should rest for a while but she is too excited. She sees plumes of smoke coming out of an enormous factory to her left and decides to make her way there. She is about halfway when she hears a car coming. She waves her arms up and down, trying to make it stop. The car slows down. The driver has rolled down the passenger window. She recognises his face. Thank God she's safe now.

'Please help me,' she says.
He nods and stretches his arm out as to welcome her in. She opens the door and falls exhausted into the passenger seat. Instinctively she leans forward to

find the seatbelt and screams. Any energy she has left streams out of her body. Lying next to her feet in the foot well of the car is a black balaclava.

'You've done it now,' the driver says and puts his foot on the accelerator.

22

It's about an hour's drive from Downham Market to Peterborough but by the time Steve gets there it is close to six o'clock. Steve and DI Woods have agreed to meet in the car park of the Great Northern Hotel for no other reason than that it is a place they both know. When he arrives, his phone pings a text message from DI Woods:

"I'm inside having a coffee."

Steve makes his way to the bar where his colleague is studying the menu.

'They do some interesting bar snacks here,' he announces.

'Go ahead then,' says Steve, 'I could do with something myself.' They make their choices and find a quiet table near the back of the room.

'How are we approaching this?' DI Woods asks.

'I'm think we're going to have to be careful. Pieters' name keeps coming up but we have absolutely no evidence he is involved in any way. So I think we'll play the missing person card and see how he reacts.'

Steve explains he has spoken to a colleague at Peterborough Police Station to make them aware of their interest in Mr Pieters and to find out if the local police have any useful information. The colleague had done a quick search but nothing significant had come up. Apparently, the police were aware the premises were occasionally used for prostitution but as there were no complaints or evidence of drug dealing or people smuggling, they had so far not taken any action.

DI Woods leaves his car in the hotel car park and joins Steve. When they arrive at the address, they park across the road and observe the building for a few minutes. What they see surprises both of them. A group of about eight to ten men have formed a queue outside. Their presence makes it difficult to look in through the shop window and see what is going on.

'Do you think they are queuing for the brothel to open?' DI Woods wonders aloud.

'If they are, they are quite blatant about it,' replies

Steve. 'Let's go, I'm intrigued.'

Rather than joining the line, they make their way to the front, apologising and explaining they are police officers. This does not deter those waiting in the queue in any way and it soon becomes clear the shop is in fact a recruitment agency and, Thursday being payday, the men are here to collect their wages. The two detectives enter the shop, show their warrant cards, and ask to speak to Mr Pieters. Without saying anything, the woman behind the desk dials a number on her phone.

'Curly, there are two policemen here to see you.' She listens for a second and then points to a door at the side of the shop.

'Upstairs,' she says.

Where the shop downstairs can best be described as shabby and in need of a facelift, the opposite is true for the rest of the building. Steve had expected a narrow staircase with a worn-out carpet, but when they open the door they find themselves in a spacious lobby, tastefully furnished with a smart modern reception desk and a wide set of stairs leading to the first floor. To the right is a door which gives direct access onto the street. When they are about to go up, they hear a door open and a thickset man appears at the top of the stairs.

'Follow me,' he says. He takes them through

174

another lobby with comfortable seats into a spacious room with a number of tables, sofas and a small bar. From there, they walk along a corridor with several rooms leading off it until they arrive at the far end, where a door stands half open and a tall man with blond hair is waiting for them.

'Thank you Teddy. I'll take it from here.'
Without saying anything, the man turns around and makes his way back.

'I'm Derk Pieters,' the blond-haired man introduces himself before going through into a small office, only big enough for a desk, a couple of filing cabinets and two chairs for visitors.

'Sorry, I can't offer you any refreshments, the bar doesn't open until ten o'clock. But how can I help you gentlemen?'
The South African accent is quite strong.
Steve introduces DI Woods and himself and produces the missing poster with Alecja's picture on it.

'We wonder if you can help us locate this person. We understand she rents her home from you.'

'I heard about the girl going missing,' Pieters replies. 'So you haven't found her yet. If you ask me, she's taken herself off and has moved somewhere else, probably back to Poland.'

'Why would she do that?'

'She's difficult. Always complains about everything. And she owes me nearly a thousand pounds in unpaid rent. If it wasn't for her cousin, I would have thrown her out a long time ago but Lena is a decent hardworking girl. I wouldn't be surprised if Alecja owed other people money as well.'

'When did you last see her?' Steve asks.

'A couple of weeks ago,' comes the reply. 'I told her in front of her cousin that if she didn't pay, she would have to leave. I actually offered her a chance to work for me here in the club.'

This is a new take on things, Steve thinks, not a brothel, a club.

'What kind of club is it?'

Pieters laughs.

'I know people describe it as a brothel but I can assure you it's nothing of the kind. What we have here is a comfortable space for discerning adults to rent and engage in whatever activities they wish to indulge. We supply the premises, staff the bar, keep the riff-raff out and do the laundry. It's all legal and entry is by invitation only.'

Clever, Steve thinks, by having different individuals taking responsibility, Mr Pieters cannot be accused of running a brothel himself.

'Okay,' he continues, 'have you seen her since?'

'Only once,' comes the reply. 'By chance outside

176

Barkas' nightclub in Wisbech. I asked her if she'd found a job yet and she started shouting at me. She was embarrassing herself, so I left. Meeting people like that is not good for my blood pressure, so I try and stay away from the likes of her. Teddy, who you met, does more and more of the rent collecting and that kind of thing for me so I can avoid getting into rows with people like her.'

'Maybe we can talk to Teddy later?' Steve suggests.

'By all means,' Pieters replies, 'but I warn you, he's a man of few words. It's why he's so good at his job. He doesn't get into arguments.'

Steve turns to DI Woods. He shakes his head, no further questions.

'Before we go, do you know Jimmy Jackson?'

Curly looks confused.

'I know Jack Jackson,' he replies, 'is he related to Jimmy?'

'Jimmy is, or rather was, his father. He was murdered the same day Ms Tobinska went missing.'

'Well, there's your answer then,' replies Pieters. 'An open-and-shut case if you ask me. The girl killed him and done a runner.'

'Can I ask how you know Jack Jackson?' Steve interjects.

'Oh, I've known him for years. I keep racehorses

and he used to be my vet. But I've moved them to stables near Oundle because it's closer for me. That's too far for Jack to travel on a regular basis, especially in an emergency. But he still does all the paperwork for me when we go to race meetings abroad.'

'I think this will do for now,' Steve says, getting up to go. 'One more thing. Is it true you have Ms Tobinska's passport?'

He notices a flicker of anger in Derk Pieter's eyes.

'Yes, I do,' comes the reply. 'Safely locked away in there,' pointing at one of the filing cabinets.

'Do you think that is acceptable?'

'It's no different to you handing over your passport in a foreign hotel,' Pieters claims. 'And they can have them back any time they need them,' he adds.

With that, he gets up and calls Teddy.

Steve drives DI Woods back to his car in the hotel car park.

'What do you think?' he asks.

'I think our Mr Pieters tries hard to present himself as a legit businessman. But in my opinion, law-abiding citizens don't need to employ a gorilla like his mate Teddy to do their dirty work for them.'

Steve nods.

'I agree,' he says. 'And they also don't need to resort to taking people's passports as security. I wouldn't be surprised if it was one of the reasons Ms Tobinska argued with him. I'm sure he knows more than he lets on. Now we know a bit more about him I think we should start digging a bit deeper.'

On leaving, Mr Pieters had given them his phone number and email address. He did indeed seem to live in a luxury motorhome rather than a house. Apparently, he was currently parked on an upmarket caravan park near Fotheringay.

They had also briefly talked to Teddy, whose real name was Sean Brown according to Mr Pieters but who had acquired the name Teddy on account of his bear-like appearance. Teddy answered 'Yes, No,' or 'I don't know.' to every single question the detectives asked him, so before long they decided they were wasting their time and made for Steve's car. After dropping DS Woods off at the car park at the Great Northern Hotel, Steve starts making his way home.

Once he has left the traffic of the city behind him, he checks the time on the dashboard display. Eight thirty. He dials Julia's number but no one picks up. Unable to text because he is driving, he leaves a voice message telling her she can ring back any time tonight. He turns on *Radio 6 Music* and settles in for the drive back home. His mind goes over the day's events. 'I wonder how Eva got on with DCS Sutton?' he thinks and dials Eva's number. After a while, her answerphone kicks in. He decides against leaving a message and terminates the call. In spite of trying to relax, he's feeling somewhat uneasy. Is it because the case appears to be going nowhere? *Or is it because straight after he rang his wife, he rang Eva?*

23

DCS Sutton is getting ready for her *Zoom* meeting. She is a little nervous as this is the first time she has used this platform but she and Maddy had had a practice earlier on in the day and she soon realised it was not much different from using *Skype*, something she does on a regular basis when talking to her mother in Western Australia. Maddie is in charge of the technical side of things, so Sarah can fully concentrate on the task at hand. The screen lights up and most of the journalists present at the first meeting appear in front of her.

'Afternoon, everyone,' Sarah welcomes them. 'In spite of some progress, we are still looking for the whereabouts of Ms Alecja Tobinska, who has not been seen since Monday morning. In addition, you will by now have heard about the unexplained death of Mr Jimmy Jackson in suspicious circumstances. One line of inquiry we are following is that the two incidents are linked. We would like to hear from anyone with further information, one way or the other. We are by now extremely concerned about the welfare of Ms Tobinska who, as I pointed out before, is most likely injured. I appeal to your readers, listeners and viewers who have seen or heard from her to contact us immediately. If they do not wish to give their name and address, they can simply contact *Crimestoppers.* Any questions?'

'What is the connection between Mr Jackson and Ms Tobinska?' someone asks.

'We are still investigating that,' DCS Sutton replies. 'We know at one point Ms Tobinska was employed by Mr Jackson but whether or not that has any bearing on the case is something we are actively pursuing.'

'How did Jimmy Jackson die?'
Sarah paused.

'I am not at liberty to reveal precise details of the manner of his death but I can say it was the result of a violent attack.'

'So,' Alan Phelan interjects, 'are you saying we have a killer in our midst? Should my readers be worried?'

'Thank you, Alan,' Sarah responds. 'We believe this was an isolated incident, a targeted attack on Mr Jackson if you like, and other than Ms Tobinska, we don't think anyone else is in immediate danger. But it goes without saying that if any of your readers suspect anyone, they should ring us and not directly approach the possible perpetrator as they might put themselves in danger.'

'Is Ms Tobinska a suspect? Do you think she attacked Mr Jackson?'

'We are following a number of lines of inquiry and have of course, considered it. We believe it is unlikely but are keeping an open mind. But it is definitely another reason why it is imperative we find Ms Tobinska as soon as possible, even if it is only to eliminate her from our investigation.'

'Is it true you have arrested Mick Mendham?' another journalist asks.

'You know we cannot reveal who we speak to or why we do so,' Sarah responds in her best, disapproving school-teacher voice. 'I would appeal to all of you that it would not be proper to publish any names at this moment in time, other than those of Ms Tobinska and Mr Jackson. Equally, I would like to thank a number of members of the public for assisting us on a voluntary basis with our inquiries. So far, no arrests have been made.'

She pauses:

'If there are no more questions, I thank you all for your help and cooperation.'

And that is it. She walks downstairs, thanks Maddy for her help and tells her to go home.

'What about you?' Maddy suggests. 'Shouldn't you go home yourself?'

'I will,' Sarah smiles. She walks back to her office, switches on the coffee machine and sits down, waiting for PC Lappinska to appear.

While Steve is on his way to Peterborough, Eva is driving back to the Jacksons'. She has taken her own car and parks it a bit further from the house as both the Range Rover and the Audi are parked, not in the garage, but in the drive nearer the house. While walking towards the front door, she hears raised voices through an open window. They've obviously not heard her arriving! Should she leave? She hesitates and hears Jack say:

'Well, it's done now. Make sure I don't forget to put the bag in the incinerator waste tomorrow.'

'What have we got ourselves into?' Marion cries.

'Nothing,' says Jack. 'Relax, it's all over.'

Eva rings the bell. After a few minutes, Marion opens the door.

'Come in,' she says. 'What can we do for you?' She's obviously been crying.

'Are you alright, Mrs Jackson?'

'I'm fine,' is the reply.

Jack joins his wife.

'Marion has taken Jimmy's death quite hard,' he says. 'She tries to put a brave face on it but inside, she's suffering. Come through.'

They make their way to the living room.

'What can we do for you?'

'I wanted to update you on the paperwork you gave to us this morning. Everything is perfectly okay and normal and you'll have it back tomorrow sometime. I'm sorry, we got off on the wrong foot a bit this morning.'

'Don't worry,' Marion replies, 'both Jack and I are under a lot of pressure, especially since Jimmy's body has been released, and we're trying to organise the funeral. Of course, we should remember that police priorities are different from our own.'

'Thank you.' says Eva, 'It must be hard for you at the moment. I'm glad you take it that way: we don't want to put extra pressure on you if we can avoid it. Do you mind if I use your loo before I go?'

'Feel free,' Marion replies. 'It's through the kitchen next to the utility room.'

Eva closes the living room door behind her and walks through the hall to the kitchen. Entering the room she sees a plastic bag lying on the kitchen table. She has a quick look inside the bag. All she sees is a small yellow container, the kind used by her diabetic father for the disposal of used insulin pens.

She finds the WC, goes inside and after waiting a minute, flushes the toilet. She walks back towards the living room. The Jacksons are waiting to say goodbye in the hall. Marion opens the front door for her and says goodbye but Jack steps out with her and walks her to her car.

'Marion tells me you're interested in music. Come, let me show you our little studio and the baby grand I've bought. It's in one of the rooms above the garage.'

Eva hesitates. It would be rude to refuse but …

'It'll only take a minute,' Jack insists.

'That would be lovely,' she replies and follows him up the outside staircase. He opens the door, moves back, and invites her in. She takes a step forward and finds herself propelled into the room by an almighty shove in the back.

'There you go, bitch,' she hears Jack say. 'That should stop you from poking your nose into other people's affairs. Do you think I didn't see you checking my bag on the kitchen table? What I do is none of your business. Oh, and I bet you were listening to Marion and me arguing, you nosy bitch. Give me your phone.'

He produces a gun.

Eva takes her phone out of her coat and chucks it as hard as she can towards Jack, hoping to hit him in the face.

186

Jack ducks.

'Stupid bitch!' he shouts. 'I thought you'd be smarter than that.'

He picks up the phone and shuts the door. Eva runs towards it but before she gets there, she can hear the key turning and realises she is trapped.

Jack makes his way back to the house. He sees Marion waiting for him. I must make sure she doesn't crack, he tells himself. He goes in and puts his arms around her. She starts crying.

'Oh Jack, what are we going to do?'

'Don't worry darling, I'll take care of everything.'

'But Jack, it's not right!'

Jack is getting annoyed.

'Listen, Marion,' he says firmly. 'I didn't want this to happen either. It's not our fault. I blame that Polish whore for everything. Without her scheming, dad would still be alive. It's all her fault. But we are where we are. That policewoman probably overheard us arguing in the kitchen and saw the syringes on the kitchen table. I'm sure she doesn't know what it all means but it won't be long before she puts two and two together and then what? We would lose everything. Don't forget, we're not doing this for ourselves but for our children's future. They shouldn't be cheated out of their inheritance.'

'You're right,' Marion says, 'it's not our fault. But

what are we going to do with her?'

'Leave it to me,' Jack says.' I'll deal with that nosy cow tomorrow. But first, you need to help me get rid of her car.'

It is well past one o'clock before they finally get to their bed. Jack had driven the car to the Forty Foot Drain while Marion followed him in the Range Rover. It took them a while to find a suitable place to get the car up the bank and they had to stop a few times when they saw headlights in the distance. But no one passed anywhere near when, after one final push, the car rolled down the bank and hit the water. It floated for a few minutes and then slowly started sinking.

'That will do nicely,' Jack said to himself before joining his wife in the other car and heading home. Walking into the house, Jack puts his hand in his pocket. Blast, he still has her phone. He meant to put it in the car but forgot. Never mind, he thinks, I'll deal with it tomorrow.

While Jack and Marion are disposing of her car, Eva looks around the room that has become her prison. It is quite spacious, with a settee, a piano and some amplifiers. On a desk is a small recording mixer. What draws her attention immediately are the walls, all covered in thick black foam. Of course, it's a studio and the walls are soundproofed. She looks up, the pitched ceiling is the same apart from a small dormer window she has no chance of reaching. She realises shouting for help is no option. No one will hear her unless they are right next to the wall. She sits down on the settee.

Why is she here? What is it she overheard that made Jack Jackson want to lock her up? And what is he planning to do with her?

Kidnapping a police officer is a serious crime and carries a long prison sentence. *Oh my God,* she suddenly realises, *he's going to kill me. Those needles! Is that how he is going to do it?*

The thoughts come clear and fast now. *Did he kill his own father? Did he kill Alecja Tobinska? I've got to get out of here! I've got to tell Steve.*

She lies down on the settee, suddenly exhausted. *'Hold it together girl!'* she tells herself. After a while, she gets up and starts examining every bit of the walls and those bits of the ceiling she can touch. She pulls off some of the foam but it doesn't come loose easily. She uses a microphone stand and taps every bit of surface she can reach and listens in the hope she can locate a cavity or duct that might offer an escape. But after a few hours, she gives up. She lies down on the settee and quietly sobs herself to sleep.

.

FRIDAY

24

Steve and DCS Sutton are meeting in her office. In spite of the excellent coffee, the mood is distinctly downcast. Steve has described his visit to Peterborough. He has explained that both he and DI Woods think Mr Pieters might well be involved in some unsavoury business practices but nothing suggests he's had a hand in either Mr Jackson's death or Ms Tobinska's disappearance.

Sarah explains she's disappointed Eva did not turn up and didn't bother ringing or texting to make her apologies.

'Strange,' Steve says, without letting on that he himself tried to ring Eva the previous night. They go downstairs to the conference room where the assembled staff are waiting. Everyone is present except for Eva. No one knows where she might be and she hasn't been in contact with anyone.

'Shall I drive past her house?' DI Starling offers. 'Maybe she's overslept or is ill.'

'Thank you,' DCS Sutton says,

While they are waiting for DI Starling to return, they discuss the response to the press conference. Nothing on *Crimestoppers,* no 999 calls, but there are a number of foul messages left on the answering machines of both Wisbech and Downham Market police stations. Almost all have racist undertones, the most common ones being *"It's obvious the Polish c*** has done it, they're all thieves and whores."* Another favourite: *"If we hadn't let the foreigners in, we wouldn't have the crime."* A waste of time, DI Sutton and Steve agree, but you never know, something might turn up.

At that moment, DI Starling rings.

'I'm outside Eva's house,' she says. 'No sign of life and her car isn't here either. I'm going to see if she has parked it in one of the side streets but I'm certain she normally parks on her drive.' She rings off.

'Right,' says Steve, 'I'm going to the Jacksons. Maybe she told them where she was going after visiting them.'

Steve drives fast and reaches the barn conversion in twenty minutes. The front door is opened by Marion. Steve notices she appears tired, with bags under her eyes.

'Good morning,' he says, 'I was wondering what time my colleague PC Lappinska left here yesterday? She was here, wasn't she?'

'Yes, she was,' Marion replies, 'twice in fact. Once in the morning with another detective and she returned in the afternoon around four o'clock on her own, so she stayed and had a cuppa with us. I was glad she'd come back because I was short with her in the morning and was able to apologise.'

'And what time did she leave?' Steve asks.

'Around five o'clock I would think. I saw her drive away.'

'Did she say where she was going?'

'I presume she was going back to Downham. I saw her turn left at the end of the drive.'

Steve walks back to his car when his phone rings. It is DI Baker.

'Steve,' he says hurriedly, 'DCS Sutton has requested a trace on Eva's phone. We've received a location. It's a veterinary practice in March. We have the address and the precise coordinates.' Steve gets in his car and sets off on the road to March. His satnav predicts it will take him twenty minutes but he does it in fifteen. He leaves his car right at the front door and runs inside. The receptionist is at first confused at his request to search the premises and calls her manager.

'Look,' Steve explains, showing them his warrant card, 'this probably sounds strange but we have reasons to believe a missing person's phone is present on these premises.'

Soon everyone cooperates. After about ten minutes, two local officers from March Police Station have joined the search. DCS Sutton certainly has pulled out all the stops. Steve tries to ring Eva's number but as on the night before, it goes to answerphone each time he rings. When nothing turns up, Steve sits down with the receptionist and together they go through the previous day's appointment list, at least the part covering the end of the day. Again nothing turns up.

'How about earlier this morning?' the receptionist suggests.

'Yes please,' says Steve. It is now nearly lunchtime. A few strokes of the keyboard and today's appointment list appears on the screen. Steve notices several cancellations.

'Why so many?' he asks.

'Oh, they are all Mr Jackson's appointments. He works here on Fridays. He came in earlier on but had to leave soon after.'

'Which room does he use?'

The room has already been searched but together with one of the March constables, they start again by systematically searching all the places a phone could be hidden such as drawers, boxes and cupboards. Nothing! What about the bins? He empties both the general bin and the recycle bin onto the floor. Again nothing! All that is left to check is a large yellow plastic bucket for the disposal of sharps and hazardous waste. Steve carefully empties the contents on a table. *Bingo!* After locating the phone, Steve immediately calls DCS Sutton. He explains all units are to start looking out for Jack Jackson.

'I don't know how or why but there's no doubt he is involved. Whichever unit is the nearest has to go to the Jackson's house and if he is in, keep him there until we arrive. Arrest him if necessary. I will make my way there myself.'

'Leave it to me,' answers Sarah, 'I'll sort it from my end. And Steve, drive carefully.'

Steve does indeed drive carefully. He's thinking. How does this fit in? What does it mean? Why did Jack Jackson have Eva's phone? His own phone rings. It's DCS Sutton.

'Two things,' she says. 'The unit checking the Jackson's house has reported there is no one there. But,' she pauses, 'a car has been recovered from the Forty Foot Drain. It could be PC Lappinska's. There's no sign of a body inside and divers are now searching the water.'

'I'm making my way there now.'

'So am I,' she responds.

Steve can hardly take it all in.

'See you there,' he says and puts his foot down on the accelerator.

25

Alecja is hardly awake when the man arrives the next day. She vaguely remembers how, the day before, he had taken her back to the little house and how she hadn't had the strength to fight him. He had been extremely angry and shouted and sworn at her before tying her to the metal poles of the bed.

'You deserve a good hiding,' he had said, 'but we better keep you looking decent. After all, no one wants to fuck an ugly whore.'

'This should stop you from trying to escape again,' he'd continued, injecting her with another dose of the drug. Producing another syringe, he had added: 'You might as well have the other half from yesterday, just to make sure you stay put.'

And now he is here again but she is hardly aware of his presence. He grabs her arm roughly.

'You bitch,' he says while slapping her in the face. 'It's all gone haywire because of you. You're no use to me anymore.'

His phone rings. He does not answer it but instead injects her with another dose. Alecja is once more swallowed up into the warm embrace of the drug. By the time he takes out yet another syringe, she has lost all awareness of her surroundings and slowly drifts off into unconsciousness.

26

Marion Jackson is at her wits' end. She held it together when DCI Culverhouse called but she can't cope anymore. She's been trying to ring Jack but he doesn't pick up his phone. She's rung the practice but all they told her was Jack had left soon after he arrived and the police were searching the building. She's made up her mind. She is going to get out. All this has gone far too far. Nobody was supposed to get hurt. And now?

The bell rings and Marion sees yet another police car in the yard. She hides in the hall where she can't be seen from the outside. After a while, the two officers leave. She has decided: she's getting away from here! She runs upstairs and quickly puts some clothes in a suitcase and picks up some of her kids' favourite toys. She chucks everything on the back seat of her car and walks back to the house. She takes a key from the hook, shuts the front door and walks up the outside staircase to the studio. She knocks.

'Stand away from the door,' she shouts. 'Wait ten minutes and then run for it.'

She turns the key and runs down the stairs to her car. She gets in and drives towards the Forty Foot Drain. In the distance, she can see the flashing lights of police cars and ambulances. *'So they found the car'* she says to herself. *'That was quick. Never mind, it should keep them busy for a while.'* She turns around and drives off in the direction of Peterborough.

Eva wakes up and immediately realises what has happened to her. She is surprised by how awake and alert she feels. She reassesses her predicament. Okay, she can't escape but she is still alive. And to kill her, which she has no doubt he is planning, Jack will have to enter the room. That will be the moment she has a chance to turn the tables. She knows she is strong. What she needs is to be prepared. She picks up the microphone stand and puts it within easy reach. As a makeshift weapon, it will have to do. She takes the only chair, puts it near the door, sits down and waits. Nothing happens. She checks her watch, it's already after lunchtime. Surely he's not planning to starve her to death? Suddenly she hears a faint sound. Someone, a female voice, is talking. She can make out a few words, 'Wait ten minutes,' and hears the key turn in the door

It is soon clear there is nothing DCI Sutton and Steve can usefully contribute by staying at the crash scene. It has been established without doubt that the car recovered from the water does indeed belong to PC Lappinska. The officer in charge has promised he will ring them if or when a body is found. Sarah and Steve walk back to their cars. The mood is sombre. Steve suggests they stop at the Jacksons' again.

'I'll follow you,' Sarah suggests.

After about fifteen minutes, they cross the busy A1101 and are driving towards Nordelph along the Silt Road. In the distance, past Jack Jackson's house, Steve sees a figure running towards Jimmy's farm. At that moment, Jack Jackson's car comes out of his own drive and also makes for the farm. Steve calls Sarah in her car.

'Did you see that?'

'I did. Slow down, something's wrong here.'

She calls for reinforcements and says to Steve,

'Let's follow.'

They leave their cars on the road and quietly make their way along the side of the track to the farm. They see the grain store door half open and hear Jack shouting.

'You stupid bitch, how the fuck did you escape?' They hear the sound of a fist and a female crying in pain.

'Shut up or I'll shoot you here and now,' Jack Jackson threatens. 'How did you get out? Never mind, I've got you now and this time, you won't get out of here, not alive anyway.'

'You'll never get away with it,' they hear Eva shout at him.'

'Shut up,' Jack repeats loudly. For a minute, it goes quiet.

Steve signals to Sarah,

'I'm going in.'

They can hear sirens in the distance.

'Wait,' whispers Sarah.

'No time,' Steve says.

Sarah nods and Steve sprints to the door and pushes it wide open. Precisely at that moment, Jack Jackson lets out an almighty scream.

'You bitch! You bitch, you'll suffer for this.'

The scene Steve and Sarah witness would almost be comical if it wasn't so serious. There is Jack with an outstretched arm trying to shake Eva off but she's got her teeth deep in the flesh of his wrist. At the same time, she is kicking Jack directly in the most sensitive part of his body. And all that with both her arms tied behind her back.

Steve steps forward. Eva sees him and lets go.

Before Jack realises what's happening, he is handcuffed. Eva sinks to the floor and starts sobbing uncontrollably. Steve walks over and puts his arms around her.

'It's alright,' he says. 'You're safe.'

'I know,' she says. 'Thanks to you.'

'Not sure about that,' DCS Sutton says, 'I think you were doing quite well on your own.'

Eva takes a deep breath.

'I knew these kickboxing lessons would come in handy sometime,' she laughs in between sobs.

The paramedics, Sally and Brian, have arrived. They explain they heard the emergency call and as they had finished at the Forty Foot Drain they decided to see if they could help. They quickly check Eva has no serious injuries before they all make their way back to the station.

After the debrief, Eva is sent home. She is told to rest and DCS Sutton has arranged for Dr Walker to visit her later in the day. She has also been in touch with HR to see what kind of support Eva is entitled to after her ordeal. DI Starling is giving Eva a lift back to her house and will check whether she needs anything in terms of food, or tea and coffee. As soon as they leave, DCS Sutton calls everyone together and reminds them PC Lappinska is now on sick leave and is not to be contacted by anyone unless she herself initiates it. Is it Steve's imagination or is she looking at him when she says this? They are, of course, allowed to send messages of support and flowers if they wish to do so.

~

Marion is arrested at her parents' home in Peterborough and taken to Downham Market Police station, where she is interviewed by DCI Culverhouse and DI Starling. She refuses the offer to have her solicitor present.

'All I want is to put this whole saga behind me and make a fresh start, just me and the children.'

'That is your choice,' Steve tells her and hands her a form to sign, confirming that she has refused the aid of a solicitor.

She explains that she and Jack are going through a tricky financial patch. The barn conversion has come out way above budget and they are seriously in debt. They have been able to borrow extra money on the basis they would at one point inherit a substantial farm. After all, Jack is the only son.

'Where did you borrow the money?' Steve asks.

'Jack knows someone he occasionally works for. Something to do with horses, I think.'

She explains that lately they have seen a change in Jimmy. He had always been a placid, contented man who went about his business in a quiet, confident manner. But the last three months had been different. He had been excited and much more animated than usual. Jack and Marion soon guessed he must have got himself a girlfriend. Marion was happy for him but Jack had taken it badly.

'It's too soon after mum,' he had said and when she pointed out it had been three years since his mother's death, they'd ended up having a bad argument. Then last Sunday night, Jimmy had come over and told them he had fallen in love with this Polish woman who used to work for him.

'Imagine that,' she says, 'a woman half his age, nothing more than a gold-digging slut,' she adds bitterly. She recalls Jack had got into an almighty row with his father and Jimmy had walked out. Marion had followed him.

'I felt bad about how the evening had gone and wanted to make amends. Mind you,' she adds, 'not that I disagreed with Jack. This woman was totally unsuitable for Jimmy. I was hoping he had found some nice elderly widow who wasn't after his money and inheritance.'

When Jimmy and she got to his car, he had taken his jacket off to put it on the back seat. Out fell a great wad of twenty-pound notes held together with a plastic band.

'He looked embarrassed,' she says. 'There must have been thousands of pounds. I asked him why he had so much money on him. He told me it was some insurance payout he received from a local farm machinery company relating to the stolen tractor. He hadn't had a chance to bank it. With that, he put the money back and drove away.'

She explains how she and Jack had sat up late into the night. Neither of them believed the insurance story. Insurance companies don't pay out in cash on a Sunday afternoon. It was clear Jimmy was involved in some unsavoury scheme, no doubt cooked up by his Polish girlfriend. He obviously needed to be protected from her. They agreed they should do everything possible to prevent this gold-digger from getting anywhere near their father ever again.

'No problem,' Jack had said. 'I know someone who can take care of her.'

'What about the money? What if he gives it all to his Polish whore?'

It was then she had remembered seeing an appointment with the solicitors on Jimmy's calendar. She told Jack about it.

'I think we've got to act quickly,' he had said.

'Leave it to me.' after which he went outside where he made a couple of phone calls. When he came back in, he'd kissed her and said, 'Don't worry love, I've got it all sorted.'

DI Starling stops the tape and Steve goes out to organise some coffees. While he is out, DI Starling repeats the offer for Marion to have a solicitor present but again she refuses. *Not very smart,* DI Starling thinks. *What if Jack gets himself some smart lawyer who blames everything on Marion?* Anyway, she's offered and that is all she can do.

After the refreshments arrive, DI Starling switches the recording equipment back on.

'Let's move on,' Steve suggests. 'Mrs Jackson, what do you know about Ms Tobinska's disappearance?'

'Nothing,' Marion responds, 'but I'm glad she's gone. I wouldn't be surprised if she was involved in Jimmy's death.'

'Thank you,' Steve replies. 'You opened the door for PC Lappinska to escape. Why did you tell her to wait ten minutes? If you wanted to set her free, why not open the door and tell her she was free to go?'

'I was panicking. I thought she might attack me or something. I wanted to get away as soon as I could, to see my children.'

'Who locked PC Lappinska in the room?'

'My husband did. I told him to let her go free but he said, "*It's too late. She knows too much.*"

'What do you think he meant by saying, *"She knows too much?"*

'PC Lappinska suddenly appeared at our door. We were arguing about everything that was happening. She probably overheard bits of it because we had left the kitchen window open for fresh air as I had burnt some bacon earlier on. Then Jack found her snooping through a bag he uses for his veterinary instruments. He was worried Miss Lappinska might put two and two together and make five.'

'What do you mean by that?' DI Starling asks.

'Jack thought she might suspect him of being involved in his father's death or the disappearance of that woman. He panicked and lost all sense of reason. Locking her up, drowning her car in the Forty Foot Drain. He lost all sense of proportion.'

'PC Lappinska has told us all she saw was a selection of hypodermic needles and syringes. We have recovered them from the practice and are testing them. Why was Jack so worried they might be found?'

'I asked him that myself. He explained that in order to make some extra money, he had been helping a couple of horse trainers by injecting their animals with steroids. If he was found out, he would be struck off and we would lose our livelihood. That is why he panicked so much.'

'Okay, Mrs Jackson, We'll leave it at that for now.' He rings for a constable who arrives almost immediately.

'Thanks,' Steve says. 'Can you take Mrs Jackson back to her cell, please.'
Marion interrupts.

'I've told you everything I know and I helped your colleague escape. I want to go home. I want to see my children.'

'I'm sorry,' Steve replies, 'but we need you to stay here for now. A further decision will be made before four o'clock tomorrow afternoon.'

'It's not fair,' Mrs Jackson shouts while the constable gently ushers her out of the room.

In the other interview room, DCS Sutton and DI Baker are not having much luck with interviewing Mr Jackson. Unlike his wife, he has insisted on calling his solicitor. This means waiting for an hour and a half before she arrives from Peterborough and another thirty minutes for Jack Jackson to bring her up to date.

The delay has, however, allowed for a quick debrief with Steve, who fills his colleagues in on the interview with Mrs Jackson. Finally, everything is ready. To his great delight, DCS Sutton has asked PC Sheldon to also be present. He is put in charge of the recording equipment. As soon as everyone is seated, Jack Jackson's solicitor speaks.

'I think you should be aware my client is planning to file charges against the Fenland Constabulary for harassment by named members of the force, at a time of great emotional turmoil for him and his wife, following the violent death of his father.'

Christ give me strength, thinks Sarah. *Here we go again. You kidnap a police officer and now want to make out it is her own fault. And we are supposed to take this seriously?*

But of course, she doesn't say any of those things. Instead, she smiles at the solicitor and says:

'Your client must do as he sees fit. But it is not why we are here and you know that. So let's get on with it.'

She nods to PC Sheldon who turns on the tape recorders. DCS Sutton introduces everyone present and with the formalities over looks directly at Jack Jackson.

'Mr Jackson, can you tell us why you imprisoned PC Lappinska?'

'Yes, I'm sorry about that. I wanted to teach her a lesson. She has been harassing us for days and I got fed up with it. But I shouldn't have done it.'

He's trying to appear all apologetic and humble, Sarah realises, but he's not fooling her.

'In that case, why did you try to kill her the next day?'

'I never tried to kill her, I just threatened her.'

'With a loaded pistol?'

'I have a licence for that gun. I need it as a vet for when an animal needs to be put down in an emergency.'

'Whether or not you have a licence is not why you are here and, to be frank, is the least of your problems. What I want to know is why point a loaded gun at someone whose hands are tied behind their back?'

'Like I said, it was to threaten her and teach her a lesson. I wasn't going to kill her.'

He is almost pleading now.

'I think the fact she is still alive has more to do with PCs Lappinska's kickboxing skills and DCI Culverhouse's intervention than anything you contributed,' DCS Sutton replies in a firm but slightly sarcastic tone.

The solicitor puts her hand up.

'Leave it,' Sarah says, 'I've finished with this part of the interview for now. Let's turn to the night before your father's death. He was over at yours for Sunday dinner if I am not mistaken?'

'Yes,' Jack nods.

'Can you speak up for the tape please?' DI Baker interjects.

'Yes,' Jack repeats.

'I also understand you and your dad had an argument. What was that all about?'

'You know the answer, so why ask the question?' Jack answers with as much confidence as he can muster.

'I like to hear it from you,' comes the reply.

'He told us he was going out with this Polish slut half his age. It's disgusting. All she is after is his money.'

'Ah yes, the money. After your dad had gone home, your wife told you about a substantial sum of cash your father was carrying. Where do you think that cash came from?'

'I have no idea,' Jack says. 'All I know is I don't want that foreign bitch to get her hands on it. I told my wife. We've got to make him see sense.'

'And how were you going to do that?'

'I wasn't sure. I rang a friend of mine for advice and he calmed me down a bit. He suggested I should go and talk to my dad the next day but by then, it was too late.'

'Who is your friend?' DI Baker asks.

'Derk Pieters, he's a client really but we've become

friendly over the years.'

'Thank you, we know what happened to your father. What about Ms Tobinska, can you tell us anything about her disappearance?'

'I didn't know she had disappeared until I saw it on the news. Good riddance if you ask me. I wouldn't be surprised if she had something to do with it. We looked all over the house for the cash my wife saw. Thousands of pounds she thought it was. We couldn't find it anywhere. No doubt the Polish bitch is spending it as we speak.'

'I don't think so,' DCS Sutton says. 'We found the money and your wife was right. It was thousands, forty thousand to be precise.'

'I thought he was going to faint when I told him that,' Sarah laughs.
She and Steve are sitting in her office. Sarah tells him that after Jack had composed himself, they had not been able to get much more out of him. When asked about the syringes PC Lappinska had seen, he told more or less the same story as his wife. And nothing new after that. They sit in silence for a while.

'Whatever the purpose of the syringes,' Steve says eventually, 'we've got him for assault and false imprisonment of a police officer, a serious offence!

As far as his wife is concerned she has been aiding and abetting him. I'm sure her sentence will be shorter, especially after she freed Eva, but still. This part is an open-and-shut case, I think.'

He pauses before continuing:

'But what about the rest? I can feel in my guts he's got something to do with his father's death and Ms Tobinska's disappearance but I can't for the life of me see what or how.'

'I agree with you about Ms Tobinska,' Sarah replies, 'but what about his father? Where does Jack Jackson fit in? Does he strike you as someone who could have instigated his own father's death?'

'Well, we know he is capable of extremely violent behaviour. Unless everybody else is right when they suggest Ms Tobinska has something to do with the murder herself, the only other people who will benefit from Jimmy Jackson's death are Jack and Marion. They are in financial trouble, they see the inheritance disappear in front of their eyes, and they are desperate. That in itself is a motive for getting rid of both Ms Tobinska and Mr Jackson. If only we could find Ms Tobinska.'

By now, it is nearly ten o'clock in the evening.

'Time to go home,' DCS Sutton suggests. 'I've been told the forensic results from the syringes, as well as some outstanding samples from the crime scene and the mobile home, should come in overnight. Let's hope they give us a clue as to what to do next. Goodnight Steve, try to get some sleep. We've had an eventful day.'

Sitting in his favourite chair, Steve pours himself a whiskey while waiting for his pizza to be delivered. An eventful day indeed, he thinks to himself. He briefly saw Jack Jackson in the corridor after his interview. He had a bandage over his wrist. It looked painful. He smiles and selects his favourite album, Tom Waits' *Closing Time.*
'I wonder how Eva is doing?' he says to himself while *I Hope That I Don't Fall in Love with You,* is playing in the background.

SATURDAY

27

The next morning Steve arrives at the office early. But not as early as DCS Sutton, who is waiting for him in the foyer.

'Good, you're here,' she greets him. 'I was about to ring you. The forensic results are in.'

She sounds excited. When they arrive at her office, she switches on her coffee machine. She points at a couple of sheets of paper next to the printer.

'See what you make of that.'

Steve walks over and starts reading the first page of the tests on the hypodermic syringes retrieved from the sharps bin in Jack Jackson's consulting room at the veterinary practice. It appears the residue found on them was not steroids, as he and his wife had claimed, but ketamine. The report provides a useful explanation:

"Ketamine is commonly known as a horse tranquilizer and is routinely used in veterinary practices as an anaesthetic, the same way it has been used on people."

'Well, that blows the Jacksons' story apart,' Steve says aloud.

'Read on,' Sarah urges him.

Page two concerns the crime scene in the grain store. Most of it is already known to Steve from the pathologist's report. There were several different sets of fingerprints. They have now been processed and compared to others on the National Police database. Most of them are unknown but there's one direct hit. A print found on the front of the tractor is a perfect match for Sean Brown, address unknown.

'Phew,' Steve whistles, 'your address might be unknown but I know where to find you! Teddy, we're coming for you!'

He gets his phone out.

'Wait,' Sarah interrupts, 'read on, there's more. Any arrests must be coordinated so nobody can be forewarned and disappear.'

'I'm sorry. I got carried away.' He turns back to the

papers. Tests on the envelope and some of the banknotes reveal three different sets of prints. Two of them belong to persons unknown.

'I suspect those two will be Mr Jackson and his daughter-in-law,' Sarah suggests. 'They both handled the money.'

It's the third name that stands out: Mick Mendham!

The last page deals with the mobile home. The blood found on the table and the floor belongs to two unknown individuals. But there are several fingerprints, again most of them unknown, except for two: Mick Mendham and Sean Brown.

'Bingo!' says Steve. 'I think we're getting there.'

DCS Sutton agrees.

'The only disappointing thing is we can't tie Jack Jackson to either of the crime scenes.'

She pours them both a coffee.

'Thank you,' Steve replies, 'but even if we had found his fingerprints at the grain store, he could easily explain them away. After all, he regularly visited the farm. I saw him there myself after his father was found. But if we had evidence he was present at the mobile home that would be different.'

'We only got Mr Jackson's prints yesterday,' Sarah replies. 'I will ask for an urgent comparison.'

They finish their coffees.

'Let's bring the others up to speed.'

There's a buzz in the conference room. At last something is happening. Steve has been on the phone with his colleagues in Peterborough. They have agreed Sean Brown's arrest will take place at eleven o'clock precisely. From the Downham end, DI Woods and DI Starling will coordinate the arrest of Mick Mendham. They will have backup in the form of PCs Redding and Sheldon while Wisbech Police will be on standby. Sergeant Newman is tasked with getting the cells and interview rooms ready. With a bit of luck, they will have four people in custody by lunchtime. Steve cannot remember it ever being so busy before. When the meeting comes to an end DI Starling stands up and says she has spoken to PC Lappinska.

'She thanks you all for the nice messages and flowers and wants you to know she is doing well. Her mother is coming to stay and look after her for a few days, which is reassuring.'

After everyone has left, Steve sits in his room. Of course he should have messaged her; everyone else has. He gets his phone out. *"I hope you had a good night's sleep,"* he writes. He stops. What is he doing? He sounds like her dad. He deletes the text and writes instead. *"Get better soon, we all miss you, Steve."* and presses send. Almost immediately, his phone pings. *"Miss you too x."*

After DCS Sutton has finished talking to the Deputy Chief Constable and discussed possible charges, she makes her way to the interview room. DCI Culverhouse and DI Baker are waiting outside.

'Mind if I sit in?' Steve asks DCS Sutton.

'Be my guest,' she replies. Sergeant Newman brings in Jack Jackson. His solicitor is already waiting in the room. When the tape is running and everyone present identified, DI Baker starts.

'Mr Jackson, is there anything else you would like to add to the statement we obtained from you yesterday?'

'No,' Jack replies sullenly.

'Maybe we should tell you a number of other people are being arrested as we speak,' interjects DCS Sutton. 'Does that change your mind?'

Before Jack can reply, his solicitor speaks.

'We should have been told about this.'

'Hold your horses,' DCS Sutton says sharply. 'We haven't arrested anyone yet; as I said, we are making arrests as we speak.'

She turns to Mr Jackson.

'So Jack, does that change your mind?'

'I hope you're arresting that Polish bitch. I've got nothing more to say.'

'In that case, there's not much more to discuss,' DCS Sutton says, before continuing: 'Jack Jackson,

I am arresting you on suspicion of assault, kidnap and false imprisonment of a serving police officer. You do not have to say anything, but it may harm your defence if you do not mention when questioned something you later rely on in court. Anything you do say may be given in evidence.'

They repeat the process with Marion Jackson, although in her case the charge is changed to *"aiding and abetting in the assault, kidnap and false imprisonment of a serving police officer."* Marion is told she is allowed to go but has to live at her parents' address, not speak to anyone involved with the case, hand over her passport and report to Peterborough Police Station every Monday morning until such time as she receives a summons to appear in court.

By eleven-thirty, Steve receives a call from Peterborough with the information that Sean Brown has been arrested. He immediately calls the number Derk Pieters has given him. Pieters answers after the first ring.

'What's all this about, you arresting my right-hand man? I need him here. Let him go as soon as you can,' Pieters demands.

Not likely, Steve thinks, but instead he says,

'I need you to make a statement. It would be best if you came to the Downham Station voluntarily but we can arrange a time at Peterborough Police Headquarters if necessary.'

'And if I refuse?'

'We'll arrest you for withholding information and obstruction in a murder inquiry.'

'I was going to London later anyway. I'm in Wisbech at the moment. I'll make a detour past Downham Market.'

Mick Mendham is sitting in an interview room. He's not happy. As soon as Steve and DI Starling enter the room, he addresses Steve directly.

'I thought better of you. Why are you arresting me? I've done nothing wrong.'

'In that case, you've got nothing to worry about,' answers Steve.

After the formalities have been completed and the tape is running, Steve explains why Mick has been arrested. He also states Mr Mendham has refused a solicitor.

'Let's start with the mobile home where the Tobinska cousins lived. Can you explain why your fingerprints were found on the door and on the edge of the worktop in the kitchen?'

'Easy,' Mick replies, 'I used to own that unit, as you know, and regularly visited it to collect the rent. Occasionally I had a coffee with them.'

'But that was quite a long time ago,' DI Starling suggests. 'Surely those prints would have disappeared by now? Are you sure you never visited them after you sold the home to Mr Pieters?'

'I might have done,' Mick replies.

'Why did you go back if you had nothing to do with them anymore?'

'I went to see Alecja, she still owed me money for unpaid rent. I had a job I needed doing and I thought she might be interested as a way of paying her debt.'

'What was the job?'

'Some land work. Nothing important. Anyway, she refused.'

DCS Sutton, in the meantime, was having a distinctly one-sided interview with Sean Brown, better known as Teddy. It wasn't that he wasn't cooperating: he simply didn't say much. He happily confirmed who he was, gave his address and said he worked for Mr Pieters. But that was it.

'Did he want a solicitor?'

'No.'

'Had he ever been to Jimmy Jackson's farm?'

'No.'

'Did he know who Jimmy Jackson was?'

'No.'

'Had he heard of Alecja Tobinska?'

'No.'

222

'Had he ever been to the caravan site in Nordelph?'
'No.'
'Can he explain why his fingerprints were found in Ms Tobinska's home in Nordelph?'
'No.'
'Did he know why he had been arrested?'
'No.'
'Had he talked to Jack Jackson?'
'No.'
'Could he explain why his fingerprints were on the tractor?'
'No.'

He was sent back to his cell.

'We'll have to wait until we get the results from forensics on his blood type,' DCS Sutton sighs.

In the other interview room, Steve has decided it's time to put a bit more pressure on Mick Mendham.

'What about your fingerprints on the banknotes found In Jimmy Jackson's car?' Could you explain this, please?

'I owed Jimmy some money and he told me he preferred it in cash.'

'It wasn't just some money, was it? Surely, it's not normal in this day and age to carry £40,000 in cash?'

'Jimmy was an old-fashioned guy,' Mick suggests. 'Maybe he didn't want the tax office to find out about it.'

'What was the money for?'

'Some farm machinery.'

'Including a tractor?'

'Yes,' Mr Mendham replies.

'Listen Mick,' Steve says to him. 'I don't know the details but I will find out. From where I'm standing, you are in deep shit. A man is murdered after you have given him £40,000 in cash. We have evidence some of that cash was meant for Ms Tobinska, who has disappeared, leaving a trail of blood. Your fingerprints are found at both crime scenes. I think it's time to come clean.'

Mick looks up,

'Can I have a solicitor, please?'

28

The four detectives meet in Sarah's office. It is two o'clock and they agree progress is slow.

'But we are getting there,' DCS Sutton insists. 'It's simply a matter of time.'

Steve agrees but before he can speak, Maddy calls him to say Derk Pieters has arrived. Steve takes him to an empty interview room accompanied by DI Woods.

'Coffee?' he offers.

'Is it any good?' comes the reply.

'I can't vouch for it,' Steve says. 'Let's get on with it.'

'Do you mind if I record the conversation?' DI Woods asks.

'Fine with me but can we be clear, I'm not under arrest, am I?'

'No,' Steve replies, 'you are here on a voluntary basis and can leave whenever you wish to. Let's start with your relationship with Jack Jackson. Would you call him a friend?'

'I suppose so,' Derk answers, 'maybe more like a good acquaintance. We don't see that much of each other but when we do, we get on well.'

'You received a phone call from Mr Jackson late on Sunday night. Care to tell us what it was about?'

'Jack was upset. That bitch Alecja had wriggled her way into his father's bed and Jack was worried she might be after his inheritance. Apparently, his wife had seen a lot of cash lying around. He asked me for advice on how to deal with the situation.'

'And what did you say?'

'I suggested he gets the money from his dad as soon as possible and pays the Polish girl to leave. I'm sure if you flashed a couple of thousand in her face, she would leave for Peterborough or Norwich like a shot.'

'But how was Jack supposed to persuade his father to give him the money?'

'I suggested he might want to simply take it. In a way it would be his money anyway in the future, so it wouldn't really be stealing. More like safeguarding.'

'How did Jack react to that?'

'He liked the idea but felt nervous of breaking into his father's house and asked if I knew someone who could do it for him.'

'And did you?'

'I gave him Teddy's number. What happened after that is none of my business.'

Steve and DI Starling are again sitting opposite Mick Mendham, who is now accompanied by his solicitor.

'Welcome,' Steve says. 'Any more to say, Mick?' His solicitor answers:

'My client would like to stress he has nothing whatsoever to do with the two violent incidents you are trying to connect him to. On fairly flimsy evidence, I must say. But he is prepared to fully explain the origins of the £40,000 cash he paid to Mr Jackson.' He nods at Mick.

'It's simple. Jimmy Jackson sold me his tractor for £40,000 and reported it stolen. It's worth more than twice that. He had it insured on a new-for-old basis, so when he got his payout from the insurance company, he was able to buy a brand new tractor. Our deal was that I would pay him the money as soon as I had sold the tractor. Well, I did two weeks ago. It's as simple as that.'

'Where does Ms Tobinska come into all this?'

'When I went to see her about the money she owes me, she told me she still had a grudge against Jimmy Jackson about sacking her. Apparently, she had been to his house to see him but he told her he had no cash. She asked me if Jimmy wanted to sell any of his machinery cheaply, would I be interested. I told her if she made that happen, her debt with me would be cleared. I suppose she went back and put the idea into Jimmy's head. The rest was easy. Jimmy drove his tractor to the docks at King's Lynn, from where Alecja picked him up in his own car. I went the next day and collected it. That way, there was supposed to be no trace of us meeting.'

They terminate the interview.

'You are free to go,' Steve tells Mick. 'You will most likely face a charge for handling stolen goods or something similar but we will be in touch about that at a later date.'

He walks Mick to the car park where his wife is waiting.

'Tell me, how do you sell a tractor without paperwork?'

'Easy, there are plenty of farmers who have two or more farms. They clone the number plate from one of their existing tractors and put it on the one they've bought cheaply. As long as it's the same model and the tractors are never in the same yard at the same time, no one will ever suspect anything.'

'One more question. In your opinion, is Alecja Tobinska a gold-digger?'

'I thought so at first,' Mick replies. 'She's highly strung and was angry with Jimmy, well with the whole world really. But I've met her a couple of times lately and there was no doubt she was happy. *"Jimmy and I have become friends,"* she told me. *"He's a lovely man."* You ask me, she might not love him but I think she really cares for him.'

'One final thing. I can find this out from forensics anyway, but why are your fingerprints on our database?'

'Ah,' Mick replies, 'the sins of my youth! A friend of mine stole a car and took it for a joyride when we were younger. When he was finished with it, I dismantled it and sold all the different parts. I was given a suspended sentence for selling stolen goods. But those days are long gone, I'm a pillock of society now,' he laughs.

Steve smiles. He is not so sure. Didn't the old guy in King's Lynn tell him that he had seen more than one tractor waiting to be collected? Maybe, but now is not the time he decides, and walks back inside.

~

'Remember,' Sarah says to Steve, 'let's make sure when this is all over we make a point of thanking everyone at Forensics. They've really come up trumps today, even though it's a Saturday.'

Steve agrees. The results of the blood tests confirmed Sean Brown's presence at both crime scenes.

'I think he must have cut his hand or his fingers on some of the cutlery or broken glass we saw in Ms Tobinska's home.'

So they now have both DNA and fingerprints, placing him directly at the scene. Derk Pieters has organised a solicitor who has spoken with "Teddy" at length before announcing that Mr Brown wishes to make a statement. With DI Baker sorting out the recording equipment, DCS Sutton and Steve wait. They expect Sean to give a brief monosyllabic statement but to their surprise, he does the opposite. He turns to his solicitor, who nods encouragingly.

'I admit I tried to steal the money from Mr Jackson,' he says. 'I was promised £1000.00 to get it. I went to the farm early in the morning, probably around five thirty. I wanted to get there before any of the workers turned up. I expected Mr Jackson to be asleep. I was told where the spare key to his house was hidden and also where the keys to the sheds were kept in the lean-to. But when I got out of my car, he stood there pointing a shotgun right at me. He told me to get into the grain store and said:

"I've had enough of you city folks coming here and thinking you can just walk in and help yourself to whatever you want."

'I walked towards the grain store.'

"Get in there," he said, *"I'm going to call the police."*

'I pretended to fall and was able to kick him. He fell over and dropped the gun. I kicked it away and dragged him inside the shed and asked him where the cash was. He refused to say. So I tied his wrists together and put a bit of rope around his neck to frighten him so he would tell me where the money was hidden. He suddenly started shaking and sweating. He had trouble breathing and then he just fell down and died. *I'm in trouble now,* I thought and panicked. I cut myself and started bleeding. I've seen a film once where a murderer tries to make it look like suicide, so I stood him up against the tractor and blew his head off. I moved his body forward a bit, so he lay flat on the ground, and put the shotgun next to him on the floor and put the keys on the hook in the lean-to and left. I went to Downham Market and had a cup of coffee at Greggs. Then the guy who promised me the money rang and asked how I got on.'

'Who was that?' Sarah asks.

'I don't know but Curly told me to trust him. I told

him what had happened and that I had tried to make it look like suicide. But I didn't tell him I shot him in the face,' Teddy continued.

'He seemed pretty upset about it and told me I was useless. But he calmed down and said I would have to make up for my mistake and told me to get to the caravan site in Salters Lode by eight o'clock. I went there and after a while, this guy in a Range Rover with blacked-out windows wearing a balaclava and surgical gloves turned up. I noticed the gloves because they looked funny.'

'How do you mean, funny?'

'I mean, he was all dressed in black but was wearing these blue rubber gloves.'

Steve saw a smile curl around Teddy's lips.

'He told me to go to this particular caravan and make sure the woman who lived there was *constrained,* as he called it. I knew who lived there because I'd been there before to collect the rent. When I knocked on the door, it wasn't the same woman I normally speak to. But I did recognise her. Curly once pointed her out to me and told me she owed him a lot of money.'

'What do you want?' she said. 'I didn't say anything but grabbed her like I was told to do. She fought back and threw cups, plates, glasses and all sorts, but in the end I got her on the floor. She cut her wrist

232

really badly from a broken glass, I think. There was blood everywhere. I sat on top of her. The guy in the balaclava came in and put a needle in her leg and she went quiet. He told me to leave and not talk to anyone about what had happened. I was glad to get away, I tell you that.'

'Do you think she was still alive when you left?'

'Oh yes, no doubt about it; I could hear her breathing.'

'I cannot believe anyone can sit there and give such a detailed account of what they've done without showing any emotion.' DI Baker says when Mr Brown is led back to his cell.

'I know what you mean,' DCS Sutton agrees. 'I don't mind saying, it made me shiver. To tell us that just after he shot a man's head off he went for a coffee at Greggs! But he gave us quite a detailed account of what happened. I have no doubt the man in the balaclava is Jack Jackson.'

'Except we have no proof,' Steve replies, 'and more importantly, we still have no idea where Alecja is or whether she's still alive.'

A WEEK LATER

29

Jack Jackson is in Norwich Prison awaiting trial for assault, kidnapping and imprisonment of a serving police officer.

Marion Jackson has been granted extended bail and is living with her parents. She has been suspended from her teaching job.

Sean Brown has been charged with GBH and manslaughter, although the charges may be amended depending on more evidence coming to light.

Mick Mendham has been told that although he will not face criminal charges, his file has been forwarded to HMRC, so he can no doubt look forward to some pretty detailed scrutiny of his financial affairs which will most likely result in a hefty tax bill.

After the confession from Sean Brown, the officers brought Jack Jackson back to the interview room. They had checked Teddy's phone but none of his numbers corresponded with Jack or Marion's mobiles.

'No doubt he used a cheap pay-as-you-go which he's chucked in the river by now,' Steve suggested. 'And he's probably burnt the balaclava.'

The room above the garage was searched and so was his car. Several unknown fibres were found but without Alecja's DNA, they couldn't make a connection. Jack Jackson simply denied any involvement or knowledge, either of his father's death or Alecja's disappearance.

Steve and Sarah are back in her office. Neither feels satisfied with the outcome. Yes, the right people are behind bars but as far as the two detectives are concerned, not finding Alecja leaves a dark cloud over the whole case.

'I thought we were so close,' Sarah says.

'I know,' Steve replies, 'I can't help feeling annoyed with myself for not suspecting Jack

Jackson sooner. After all, we both know that most murders are committed by family members or other close friends. I think I was fooled because he seemed so genuinely upset after seeing his father lying dead in the grain store.'

'I agree,' Sarah replies. 'I feel the same but there is no point in beating ourselves up over it. Let's learn from it and use it as a reminder if a similar situation arrives.'

'Thanks,' says Steve. It is what he needed to hear.

'But I can't stop thinking that until we know what happened to Alecja we have not solved the case.'

'Let's go home,' Sarah suggests. 'I know we will find her one day.'

Steve makes himself a spaghetti bolognese in the kitchen back home. He's listening to *Absolute Radio*. He needs loud music, probably to drown out the disappointment he feels inside. He opens a bottle of red and sits down to eat his dinner. His phone rings. It's Julia. She sounds upbeat.

'Can we meet tomorrow?' she asks. 'I thought Cambridge for lunch, halfway for both of us.'

'Great,' he replies, 'what about the boys?'

'Just you and me, I think,' she replies.

'We need to talk.'

EPILOGUE

Two months after the disappearance of Alecja Tobinska, six members of the Broomhill Dangerous Sports Club set off from Stoke Ferry for their annual canoe trip to the village of Hilgay, ten miles downstream on the River Wissey. In spite of the impressive sounding name, the only dangerous activity these sixty-plus-year-olds engage in is drinking too much alcohol and telling too many dodgy jokes.

Today is to be no different. The three canoes are laden with essentials: sandwiches, towels (they regularly fall in the water) and most importantly, several six-packs of assorted beers and lagers. They make their way down the river and by lunchtime, pass the impressive Wissington Sugar Beet Factory, at one point the largest in Western Europe. Half a mile past the factory, they stop at a small inlet in front of an old abandoned pump house. An ideal place for some lunch and the first of many drinks of the day. Or so they think. After a while, two of them decide to have a closer look at the building and notice a brand new bolt on the outside of the door. They slide it open and enter the interior, where they are surprised to see a camp bed complete with bedding and a pillow. On the bed, they find the decomposing remains of what later turns out to be a young woman. They've suddenly gone off their lunch and quickly make their way outside and rejoin the others. Together they wait for the police to arrive.

Steve and Sarah are convinced the body must be that of Alecja Tobinska. DI Starling has taken Lena to the mortuary in King's Lynn, where she identifies different items of clothing and a watch as belonging to her cousin. Unsurprisingly she breaks down and once again, DI Starling finds herself comforting Lena over a coffee.

'How do I tell my uncle and aunt?' she cries. 'They will be heartbroken.'

'Do you want us to do it?' DI Starling offers.

'No,' Lena replies, 'it is better if they hear it from me.'

A few days later, the pathologist confirms a positive identification after comparing dental records matching those of the body found in the pump house. She promises a full report will follow as soon as she has completed it.

When the report arrives, it does indeed include a lot of useful detail. By the time Alecja's body was found, she had been dead for roughly two months. Her hands and feet had been tied to the bed, so she would not have been able to move. The cause of death was most likely starvation, although according to the pathologist, she would not necessarily have suffered as she was found with unnaturally high levels of ketamine in her body which would almost certainly have induced an extended coma. Interestingly they also found several unknown fibres on the body and a syringe with fingerprints on it. Whoever murdered her must have been either in a great hurry or extremely careless.

It only took two days of intensive lab work to establish that the fibres found in Jack Jackson's car and in the room above the garage matched those of Alecja Tobinska. What is more, his fingerprints and DNA were found directly on the body.

'Bingo!' Steve says when he receives the report, but he sounds more upbeat than he actually feels. Before long, DCS Sutton and he are on their way to Norwich. On arrival, they are met by Mr Jackson's solicitor.

'Jack wants to come clean,' he tells them. 'The interview should be no more than a formality.'

In the end, it takes longer than expected. Defiant as ever, Jack Jackson admits to kidnapping Alecja, keeping her in his studio for a night before moving her to the pump house. But according to him, he visited her every day with food, had dressed her wrist, which had gone septic, and generally looked after her well.

'What about the ketamine?'

'That was her choice. She begged me to give it to her. She told me it made her feel warm inside.'

'Why did you tie her up?'

'I didn't.'

'Why didn't you kill her immediately rather than make her suffer?' DCS Sutton asks.

'I didn't want her dead. I was promised that if I kept her alive, I would get good money for her from some people Curly knows. And she owed me that. Because of her, I lost everything. My father, my inheritance, my freedom.'

'I almost thought he wanted us to feel sorry for him,' Sarah remarks on the way home, 'The bastard,' she adds.

Steve looks up. He's rarely heard her swear before.

'Imagine,' Sarah continues. 'If he had told us this on the day we arrested him, Alecja might still be alive.'

'I agree,' Steve says, before making a phone call.

Not long after they get back to Downham Market, a police car from Peterborough with a handcuffed Derk Pieters in the back arrives in the car park.

'Mr Pieters,' Steve explains, 'people smuggling, forced prostitution, threatening behaviour and facilitating or instigating criminal acts are all serious offences. Are you aware of that?'

'I am,' Curly smiles. 'That's why we have coppers like yourself to make sure these things don't happen.' And that was more or less it. Derk Pieters agreed with everything Steve threw at him. Yes, he had suggested to Jack Jackson that Teddy might be a useful person to talk to, yes he did agree some girls and their minders could make a lot of money out of prostitution but he himself was not involved in any of that. And unless they could prove otherwise, he should be let go. In the end, they had no choice but to do just that. When they told him he was free to go, he stood up, smiled at Steve and offered him his outstretched hand. Steve shook it reluctantly.

'No hard feelings, Detective Chief Inspector. 'I know you're only doing your job. By the way, don't worry about giving me a lift back to Peterborough. I'd rather take a taxi.'

Jack Jackson stands trial the following September. The charges now include a second count of false imprisonment, administering drugs without consent, kidnap and murder. He is sentenced to life in prison. He maintains throughout that his wife knew nothing of his involvement with Alecja until he told her in the conversation overheard by PC Lappinska. As a consequence, his wife's charges remain unchanged. She is given a suspended two-year custodial sentence.

Sean Brown is sentenced to 16 years in prison for his part in the death of Jimmy Jackson and the attack on Alecja Tobinska.

After the last day of the trial, Lena and DI Starling are having a coffee.

'What will you do now?'

'I'm going back to Poland,' Lena replies.

'I am so sorry that it all went so terribly wrong for you and Alecja.'

'So am I. But things will be better back home. I know there are a lot of good people like yourself in England but back home is where I belong.'

The night after the trial, Steve sits in his favourite chair with a brand new unopened bottle of Bushmills next to him. For once, he can't think of what music to put on. He pours himself a glass and let his mind drift. Could they have done better? Maybe, but really, as DCS Sutton had told him during the drive home from Norwich:

'Don't dwell on what we could have done. Let's be pleased that we've put away some dangerous criminals and have gotten some kind of justice for Ms Tobinska.'

In a different way, Curly had said the same: *"You're only doing your job."*

'*Yes, Curly,*' Steve finds himself saying out loud. *'I'm only doing my job and you better watch out because one day I'm coming for you.'*

His mind drifts further. A job which is costing him his marriage. Meeting Julia that day in Cambridge sort of sealed it. She had been matter-of-fact.

'It's not working,' she had said. 'I think we should separate. We both need to move on.'

He had agreed, partly because he realised that arguing about it would be futile but also because deep down inside he knew she was right. They had drifted apart and the physical distance between them didn't help matters. But what now? He looks at his watch. It's late, eleven thirty. He gets his phone out, finds Eva's number and sends her a text:

"Do you fancy a walk in Shouldham Forest and a pub lunch tomorrow?"

Five minutes later, the reply arrives.

"That would be lovely, thank you x."